
★

"I WANT THE CHOCOLATE-ALMOND CLUSTERS."

"They're yours," Mother assured me as she opened the white-and-black box of candies. "You know I only like the creams...hmm. No note. That's odd."

"I guess Dad just remembered how much you liked them," I offered, but it was a weak offering. This was an impulse gift. And my father never did impulsive things.

"It's been so long," Mother mused as she surveyed the open box. She finally sighed and lifted a piece. "Aurora, isn't this the one with caramel filling?"

I peered at the chocolate in question. I was sitting down, Mother was standing up, so I could see what she hadn't. There was a hole in the bottom of the chocolate. Abruptly I leaned forward and pulled another chocolate out of its paper frill. It was a nut cluster and it was pristine. Just in case, I picked up another cream. It had a hole in the bottom, too.

"Mom, put the candy down. Put it *down*. Something's wrong."

★

"Real Murders is the first adventure for Harris's perceptive protagonist and I eagerly look forward to the second." —Carolyn G. Hart

"A bright, funny and appealing heroine, and a chilling, compulsively readable plot."
—Dean James, Manager of Murder by the Book

R · E · A · L
MURDERS

CHARLAINE HARRIS

WORLDWIDE®

TORONTO • NEW YORK • LONDON
AMSTERDAM • PARIS • SYDNEY • HAMBURG
STOCKHOLM • ATHENS • TOKYO • MILAN
MADRID • WARSAW • BUDAPEST • AUCKLAND

REAL MURDERS

A Worldwide Mystery/September 1992

This edition is reprinted by arrangement with Walker and Company.

ISBN 0-373-26104-7

To Mother and Father

ONE

"TONIGHT I WANT TO tell you about that most fascinating of murder mysteries, the Wallace case," I told my mirror Enthusiastically.

I tried Sincere after that; then Earnest.

My brush caught in a tangle. "Shoot!" I said, and tried again.

"I think the Wallace case can easily fill our whole program tonight," I said Firmly.

We had twelve regular members, which worked out well with twelve programs a year. Not all cases could fill up a two-hour program, of course. Then the member responsible for presenting the Murder of the Month, as we jokingly called it, would have a guest speaker—someone from the police department in the city, or a psychologist who treated criminals, or the director of the local rape crisis center. Once or twice, we'd watched a movie.

But I'd come up lucky in the draw. There was more than enough material on the Wallace case, yet not so much that I'd be compelled to hurry over it. We'd allocated two meetings for Jack the Ripper. Jane Engle had taken one for the victims and the circumstances surrounding the crimes and Arthur Smith had taken another on the police investigation and the suspects. You can't skimp Jack.

"The elements of the Wallace case are these," I continued. "A man who called himself Qualtrough, a chess tournament, an apparently inoffensive woman named Julia Wallace, and of course the accused, her husband, William Herbert Wallace himself." I gathered all my hair into a brown switch and debated whether to put it in a roll on the back of my head, braid it, or just fasten a band around it to keep it off my face. The braid. It made me feel artsy and intellectual. As I divided my hair into clumps, my eyes fell on the framed studio portrait of my mother she'd given me on my last birthday with an offhand, "You said you wanted one." My mother, who looks a lot like Lauren Bacall, is at least five-foot six, elegant to her fingertips, and has built her own small real estate empire. I am four-foot eleven, wear big round tortoise-rimmed glasses, and have fulfilled my childhood dream by becoming a librarian. And she named me Aurora, though to a woman herself baptized Aida, Aurora may not have seemed so outrageous.

Amazingly, I love my mother.

I sighed, as I often do when I think of her, and finished braiding my hair with practiced speed. I checked my reflection in the big mirror; brown hair, brown glasses, brown eyes, pink cheeks (artificial), and good skin (real). Since it was, after all, Friday night, I'd shucked my work clothes, a plain blouse and skirt, and opted for a snug white knit top and black slacks. Deciding I wasn't festive enough for William Herbert Wallace, I tied a yellow ribbon around the top of my braid and pulled on a yellow sweater.

A look at the clock told me it was finally time to go. I slapped on some lipstick, grabbed my purse, and bounded down the stairs. I glanced around the big den/dining/kitchen area that took up the back half of the ground floor of the townhouse. It was neat; I hate to come home to a messy place. I tracked down my notebook and located my keys, muttering facts about the Wallace case all the while. I had thought about xeroxing the indistinct old pictures of Julia Wallace's body and passing them out to show the murder scene, but I decided that would perhaps be ghoulish and certainly disrespectful to Mrs. Wallace.

A club like Real Murders seemed odd enough to people who didn't share our enthusiasms, without adding the charge of ghoulishness. We kept a low profile.

I flipped on the outside light as I shut the door. It was already dark this early in spring; we hadn't switched to daylight savings time yet. In the excellent light over the back door, my patio with its high privacy fence looked swept and clean, the rose trees in their big tubs just coming into bud.

"Heigh ho, heigh ho, it's off to crime I go," I hummed tunelessly, shutting the gate behind me. Each of the four townhouses 'owns' two parking spaces: there are extra ones on the other side of the lot for company. My neighbor two doors down, Bankston Waites, was getting into his car, too.

"I'll see you there," he called. "I've got to pick up Melanie first."

"Okay, Bankston. Wallace tonight!"

"I know. We've been looking forward to it."

I started up my car, courteously letting Bankston leave the lot first on his way to pick up his lady fair. It did cross my mind to feel sorry for myself that Melanie Clark had a date and I always arrived at Real Murders by myself, but I didn't want to get all gloomy. I would see my friends and have as good a Friday night as I usually had. Maybe better.

As I backed up I noticed that the townhouse next to mine had bright windows and an unfamiliar car was parked in one of its assigned spaces. So that was what Mother's message taped to my back door had meant.

She'd been urging me to get an answering machine, since the townhouse tenants (her tenants) might need to leave me (the resident manager) messages while I was at work at the library. Actually, I believe my mother just wanted to know she could talk to me while I wasn't even home.

I'd had the townhouse next door cleaned after the last tenants left. It had been in perfect condition to show, I reassured myself. I'd go meet the new neighbor tomorrow, since it was my Saturday off.

I drove up Parson Road far enough to pass the library where I worked, then turned left to get to the area of small shops and filling stations where the VFW Hall was. I was mentally rehearsing all the way.

But I might as well have left my notes at home.

TWO

REAL MURDERS MET IN the VFW Hall and paid the Veterans a small fee for the privilege. The fee went into a fund for the annual VFW Christmas party, so everyone was pleased with our arrangement. Of course the building was much larger than a little group like Real Murders needed, but we did like the privacy.

A VFW officer would meet a club member at the building thirty minutes before the meeting and unlock it. That club member was responsible for restoring the room to the way we'd found it and returning the key after the meeting. This year the "opening" member was Mamie Wright, since she was vice president. She would arrange the chairs in a semi-circle in front of the podium and set up the refreshments table. We rotated bringing the refreshments.

I got there early that evening. I get almost everywhere early.

There were already two cars in the parking lot, which was tucked behind the small building and had a landscaped screening of crepe myrtles, still grotesquely bare in the early spring. The arc lamps in the lot had come on automatically at dusk. I parked my Chevette under the glow of the lamp nearest the back door. Murder buffs are all too aware of the dangers of this world.

As I stepped into the hall, the heavy metal door clanged shut behind me. There were only five rooms in the building; the single door in the middle of the wall to my left opened into the big main room, where we held our meetings. The four doors to my right led into a small conference room, then the men's, the ladies', and, at the end of the corridor, a small kitchen. All the doors were shut, as usual, since propping them open required more tenacity than any of us were able to summon. The VFW Hall had been constructed to withstand enemy attack, we had decided, and those heavy doors kept the little building very quiet. Even now, when I knew from the cars outside that there were at least two people here, I heard nothing.

The effect of all those shut doors in that blank corridor was also unnerving. It was like a little beige tunnel, interrupted only by the pay phone mounted on the wall. I recalled once telling Bankston Waites that if that phone rang, I'd expect Rod Serling to be on the other end, telling me I had now entered the "Twilight Zone." I half smiled at the idea and turned to grasp the knob of the door to the big meeting room.

The phone rang.

I swung around and took two hesitant steps toward it, my heart banging against my chest. Still nothing moved in the silent building.

The phone rang again. My hand closed around it reluctantly.

"Hello?" I said softly, and then cleared my throat and tried again. "Hello," I said firmly.

"May I speak to Julia Wallace, please?" The voice was a whisper.

My scalp crawled. "What?" I said shakily.

"Julia . . ." whispered the caller.

The other phone was hung up.

I was still standing holding the receiver when the door to the women's room opened and Sally Allison came out.

I shrieked.

"God almighty, Roe, I don't look that bad, do I?" Sally said in amazement.

"No, no, it's the phone call . . ." I was very close to crying, and I was embarrassed about that. Sally was a reporter for the Lawrenceton paper, and she was a good reporter, a tough and intelligent woman in her late forties. Sally was the veteran of a runaway teen-age marriage that had ended when the resulting baby was born. I'd gone to high school with that baby, named Perry, and now I worked with him at the library. I loathed Perry; but I liked Sally at lot, even if sometimes her relentless questioning made me squirm. Sally was one of the reasons I was so well-prepared for my Wallace lecture.

Now she elicited all the facts about the phone call from me in a series of concise questions that led to a sensible conclusion; the call was a prank perpetrated by a club member, or maybe the child of a club member, since it seemed almost juvenile when Sally put it in her framework.

I felt somehow cheated, but also relieved.

Sally retrieved a tray and a couple of boxes of cookies from the small conference room. She'd deposited them there, she explained, when she entered and suddenly felt the urgency of the two cups of coffee she'd had after supper.

"I didn't even think I could make it across the hall into the big room," she said with a roll of her tan eyes.

"How's life at the newspaper?" I asked, just to keep Sally talking while I got over my shock.

I couldn't dismiss the phone call as lightly and logically as Sally. As I trailed after her into the big meeting room, half listening to her account of a fight she'd had with the new publisher, I could still taste the metallic surge of adrenaline in my mouth. My arms had goosepimples, and I pulled my sweater tightly around me.

As she arranged the cookies on her tray, Sally began telling me about the election that would be held to select someone to fill out the term of our unexpectedly deceased mayor. "He keeled over right in his office, according to his secretary," she said casually as she realigned a row of Oreos. "And after having been mayor only a month! He'd just gotten a new desk." She shook her head, regretting the loss of the mayor or the waste of the desk, I wasn't sure which.

"Sally," I said before I knew I was going to, "where's Mamie?"

"Who cares?" Sally asked frankly. She cocked one surprised eyebrow at me.

I knew I should laugh, since Sally and I had discussed our mutual distaste of Mamie before, but I didn't bother. I was beginning to be irritated with Sally, standing there looking sensible and attractive in her curly bronze permanent, her well-worn expensive suit, and her well-worn expensive shoes.

"When I pulled in the parking lot," I said quite evenly, "there were two cars, yours and Mamie's. I recognized Mamie's, because she's got a Chevette like mine, but white instead of blue. So you are here and I am here, but where is Mamie?"

"She's set the chairs up right and made the coffee," Sally said after looking around. "But I don't see her purse. Maybe she ran home for something."

"How'd she get past us?"

"Oh, I don't know." Sally was beginning to sound irritated with me, too. "She'll show up. She always does!"

And we both laughed a little, trying to lose our displeasure with each other in our amusement at Mamie

Wright's determination to go to everything her husband attended, be in every club he joined, share his life to the fullest.

Bankston Waites and his light of love, Melanie Clark, came in as I put my notebook on the podium and slid my purse underneath it. Melanie was a clerk at Mamie's husband's insurance office, and Bankston was a loan officer at Associated Second Bank. They'd been dating about a year, having become interested in each other at Real Murders meetings, though they'd gone through Lawrenceton High School together a few years ahead of me without striking any sparks.

Bankston's mother had told me last week in the grocery store that she was expecting an interesting announcement from the couple any day. She made a particular point of telling me that, since I'd gone out with Bankston a few times over a year ago, and she wanted me to know he was going to be out of circulation. If she was waiting in suspense for that interesting announcement, she was the only one. There wasn't anyone in Lawrenceton Bankston and Melanie's age left for them to marry, except each other. Bankston was thirty-two, Melanie a year or two older. Bankston had scanty blond hair, a pleasant round face, and mild blue eyes; he was Mr. Average. Or at least he had been; I noticed for the first time that his shoulder and arm muscles were bulging underneath his shirt sleeves.

"Have you been lifting weights, Bankston?" I asked in some amazement. I might have been more interested if he'd shown that much initiative when I'd dated him.

He looked embarrassed but pleased. "Yeah, can you tell a difference?"

"I certainly can," I said with genuine admiration. It was hard to credit Melanie Clark with being the motivation for such a revolutionary change in Bankston's sedentary life, but undoubtedly she was. Perhaps her absorption in him could be all the more complete since she had no family to claim her devotion. Her parents, both 'only' children, had been dead for years—her mother from cancer, her father hit by a drunk driver.

Right now Melanie the motivator was looking miffed.

"What do you think about all this, Melanie?" I asked hastily.

Melanie visibly relaxed when I acknowledged her proprietorship. I made a mental note to speak carefully around her, since Bankston lived in one of "my" townhouses. Melanie must surely know Bankston and I had gone out together and it would be too easy for her to build something incorrect out of a landlady-tenant relationship.

"Working out's done wonders for Bankston," she said neutrally. But there was an unmistakable cast to her words. Melanie wanted me to get a specific message, that she and Bankston were having sex. I was a little shocked at her wanting me to know that. There was a gleam in her eyes that made me realize Melanie had banked fires under her sedate exterior. Under the straight dark hair conservatively cut, under the plain dress, Melanie was definitely feeling her oats. Her hips and bosom were heavy, but suddenly I saw them as Bankston must, as fertility symbols instead of liabilities. And I had a further revelation; not only were Bankston and Melanie having sex, they were having it often and exotically.

I looked at Melanie with more respect. Anyone who could pull the wool over the collective eye of Lawrenceton as effectively as Melanie had earned it.

"There was a phone call before you got here," I began, and they focused on me with interest. But before I could tell them about it, I heard a luscious ripple of laughter from the opening door. My friend Lizanne Buckley came in, accompanied by a very tall red-haired man. Seeing Lizanne here was a surprise. Lizanne didn't read a book from one year to the next, and her hobbies, if she had any, did not include crime.

"What on earth is she doing here?" Melanie said. She seemed really put out, and I decided we had here another Mamie Wright in the making.

Lizanne (Elizabeth Anna) Buckley was the most beautiful woman in Lawrenceton. Without Lizanne

exerting herself in the slightest (and she never did) men
would throw themselves on the floor for her to saunter on; and saunter she would, calm and smiling, never
looking down. She was kind, in her passive, lazy way;
and she was conscientious, so long as not too much
was demanded of her. Her job as receptionist and
phone answerer at the Power and Light Company was
just perfect for her—and for the utility company. Men
paid their bills promptly and smilingly, and anyone
who got huffy over the telephone was immediately
passed to someone higher on the totem pole. No one
ever sustained a huff in person. It was simply impossible for ninety percent of the population to remain
angry in Lizanne's presence.

But she required constant entertainment from her
dates, and the tall red-haired man with the beaky nose
and wire-rimmed glasses seemed to be making heavy
weather of it.

"Do you know who he is, the man with Lizanne?"
I asked Melanie.

"You don't recognize him?" Melanie's surprise was
a shade overdone.

So I was supposed to know him. I re-examined the
newcomer. he was wearing slacks and a sport coat in
light brown, and a plain white shirt; he had huge
hands and feet, and his longish hair flew around his
head in a copper nimbus. I had to shake my head.

"He's Robin Crusoe, the mystery writer," Melanie said triumphantly.

The insurance clerk beats the librarian in her own bailiwick.

"He looks different without the pipe in his mouth," John Queensland said from behind my right shoulder. John, our wealthy real-estate-rich president, was immaculate as usual; an expensive suit, a white shirt, his creamy white hair smooth and the part sharp as an arrow. John had become more interesting to me when he'd started dating my mother. I felt there must be substance below the stuffed-shirt exterior. After all, he was a Lizzie Borden expert...and he believed she was innocent! A true romantic, though he hid it well.

"So what's he doing here?" I asked practically. "With Lizanne."

"I'll find out," said John promptly. "I should greet him anyway, as club president. Of course visitors are welcome, though I don't believe we've ever had any before."

"Wait, I need to tell you about this phone call," I said quickly. The newcomer had distracted me. "When I came in a few minutes ago—"

But Lizanne had spotted me and was swaying over to our little group, her semi-famous escort in tow.

"Roe, I brought you all some company tonight," Lizanne said with her agreeable smile. And she introduced us all around with facility, since Lizanne knows everyone in Lawrenceton. My hand was engulfed in the writer's huge boney one, and he really shook it, too. I liked that; I hate it when people just kind of press your hand and let it drop. I looked up and up at his crinkly mouth and little hazel eyes, and I just liked him altogether.

"Roe, this is Robin Crusoe, who just moved to Lawrenceton," Lizanne said. "Robin, this is Roe Teagarden."

He gave me an appreciative smile but he was with Lizanne, so I realistically built nothing on that.

"I thought Robin Crusoe was a pseudonym," Bankston murmured in my ear.

"I did too," I whispered, "but apparently not."

"Poor guy, his parents must have been nuts," Bankston said with a snigger, until he remembered from my raised eyebrows that he was talking to a woman named Aurora Teagarden.

"I met Robin when he came in to get his utilities turned on," Lizanne was telling John Queensland. John was saying all the proper things to Robin Crusoe, glad to have such a well-known name in our little town, hope you stay a while, ta-dah ta-dah ta-dah. John edged Robin over to meet Sally Allison who was chatting with our newest member, a police officer named Arthur Smith. If Robin was built tall and lanky, Arthur was short and solid, with coarse curly pale hair and the flat confrontive stare of the bull who knows he has nothing to fear because he is the toughest male on the farm.

"You're lucky to have met such a well-known writer," I said enviously to Lizanne. I still wanted to tell someone about the phone call, but Lizanne was hardly the person. She sure didn't know who Julia Wallace was. And she didn't know who Robin Crusoe was either, as it turned out.

"Writer?" she said indifferently. "I'm kind of bored."

I stared at her incredulously. Bored by Robin Crusoe?

One afternoon when I'd been at the Power and Light Company paying my bill, she'd told me, "I don't know what it is, but even when I pretty much like a man, after I date him a while, he gets to seem kind of tiresome. I just can't be bothered to act interested anymore, and then finally I tell him I don't want to go out anymore. They always get upset," she'd added, with a philosophical shake of her shining dark hair. Lovely Lizanne had never been married, and lived in a tiny apartment close to her job, and went home to her parents' house for lunch every day.

Robin Crusoe, desirable writer, was striking out with Lizanne even now. She looked—sleepy.

He reappeared at her side.

"Where do you live in Lawrenceton?" I asked, because the newcomer seemed dolefully aware he wasn't making the grade with our local siren.

"Parson Road. A townhouse. I'm camping there until my furniture comes, which it should do tomorrow. The rent here is so much less for a nicer place than I could find anywhere in the city close to the college."

Suddenly I felt quite cheerful. I said, "I'm your landlady," but after we'd talked about the coincidence for a moment, a glance at my watch unsettled me. John Queensland was making a significant face at me over Arthur Smith's shoulder. Since he was president, he had to open the meeting, and he was ready to start.

I glanced around, counting heads. Jane Engle and LeMaster Cane had come in on each other's heels and were chatting while preparing their coffee cups. Jane was a retired school librarian who substituted at both the school and the public libraries, a surprisingly sophisticated spinster who specialized in Victorian murders. She wore her silver hair in a chignon, and never never wore slacks. Jane looked sweet and fragile as aged lace, but after thirty years of school children she was tough as a marine sergeant. Jane's idol was Madeleine Smith, the highly sexed young Scottish poisoner, which sometimes made me wonder about Jane's past. LeMaster was our only black member, a stout middle-aged bearded man with huge brown eyes who owned a dry cleaning business. LeMaster was most interested in the racially motivated murders of the sixties and early seventies, the Zebra murders in San Francisco and the Jones-Piagentini shooting in New York, for example.

Sally's son Perry Allison had come in too, and had taken a seat without speaking to anyone. Perry had not actually joined Real Murders, but he had come to the past two meetings, to my dismay. I saw quite enough of him at work. Perry showed a rather unnerving knowledge of modern serial murderers like the Hillside Stranglers and the Green River killer, in which the motivation was clearly sexual.

Gifford Doakes was standing by himself. Unless Gifford brought his friend Reynaldo, this was a pretty common situation, since Gifford was openly interested in massacres—St. Valentine's Day, the Holocaust, it didn't make any difference to Gifford Doakes. He liked piled bodies. Most of us were involved in Real Murders for reasons that would probably bear the light of day; gosh, who doesn't read the articles about murders in the newspaper? But Gifford was another story. Maybe he'd joined our club with the idea that we swapped some sickening sort of bloody pornography, and he was only sticking with the club in the hope that soon we'd trust him enough to share with him. When he brought Reynaldo, we didn't know how to treat him. Was Reynaldo a guest, or Gifford's date? A shade of difference there, and one which had us all a little anxious, especially John Queensland, who felt it his duty as president to speak to everyone in the club.

And Mamie Wright wasn't anywhere in the room.

If Mamie had been here long enough to set up the chairs and make the coffee, and her car was still in the parking lot, then she must be here somewhere. Though I didn't like Mamie, her non-appearance was beginning to seem so strange that I felt obliged to pin down her whereabouts.

Just as I reached the door, Mamie's husband Gerald came in. He had his briefcase under his arm and he looked angry. Because he looked so irate, and because I felt stupid for being uneasy, I did a strange thing; though I was searching for his wife, I let him pass without speaking.

The hall seemed very quiet after the heavy door shut off the hum of conversation. The white-with-speckles linoleum and beige paint almost sparkled with cleanliness under the harsh fluorescent lights. I was praying the phone wouldn't ring again as I looked at the four doors on the other side of the hall. With a fleeting, absurd image of "The Lady or the Tiger" I went to my right to open the door to the small conference room. Sally had told me she'd already been in the room, but just to temporarily park the tray of cookies, so I checked the room carefully. Since there was practically nothing to examine except a table and chairs, that took seconds.

I opened the next door in the hall, the women's room, even though Sally had also been in there. Since there were only two stalls, she'd have been pretty sure to know of Mamie's presence. But I bent over to look under the doors. No feet. I opened both doors. Nothing.

I didn't quite have the guts to check the adjoining men's room, but since Arthur Smith entered it while I hesitated, I figured I'd hear about it soon if Mamie was in there.

I moved on, and out of all the glaring beigeness I caught a little glimpse of something different, so I looked down at the base of the door and saw a smear. It was red-brown.

The separate sources of my uneasiness suddenly coalesced into horror. I was holding my breath when my hand reached out to open that door to the last room, the little kitchen used for fixing the refreshments...

...and saw an empty turquoise shoe upright on its ridiculous high heel, right inside the door.

And then I saw the blood spattered everywhere on the shining beige enamel of the stove and refrigerator.

And the raincoat.

Finally I made myself look at Mamie. She was so dead. Her head was the wrong shape entirely. Her dyed black hair was matted with clots of her blood. I thought, the human body is supposed to be ninety percent water, not ninety percent blood. Then my ears were buzzing and I felt very weak, and though I knew I was alone in the hall, I felt the presence of something horrible in that kitchen, something to dread. And it was not poor Mamie Wright.

I heard a door swoosh shut in the hall. I heard Arthur Smith's voice say, "Miss Teagarden? Anything wrong?"

"It's Mamie," I whispered, though I'd intended a normal voice. "It's Mrs. Wright." I ruined the effect of all this formality by simply folding onto the floor. My knees seemed to have turned to faulty hinges.

He was behind me in an instant. He half-bent to help me up but was frozen by what he saw over my head.

"Are you sure that's Mamie Wright?" he asked.

The working part of my brain told me Arthur Smith was quite right to ask. Perhaps coming on this unsuspicious, I would have wondered too. Her eye—oh my God, her eye.

"She's missing from the big room, but her car is outside. And that's her shoe." I managed to say that with my fingers pressed to my mouth.

When Mamie had first worn them, I'd thought those shoes the most poisonous footwear I'd ever seen. I hate turquoise anyway. I let myself enjoy thinking about hating turquoise. It was a lot more pleasing than thinking about what was right in front of me.

The policeman stepped over me very carefully and squatted with even more care by the body. He put his fingers against her neck. I felt bile rise up in my throat—no pulse, of course. How ridiculous! Mamie was so dead.

"Can you stand up?" he asked after a moment. He dusted his fingers together as he rose.

"If you help."

Without further ado, Arthur Smith hauled me to my feet and out the doorway in one motion. He was very strong. He kept one arm around me while he shut the door. He leaned me against that door. Deep blue eyes looked at me consideringly. "You're very light," he said. "You'll be all right for a few seconds. I'm going to use the phone right here on the wall."

"Okay." My voice sounded weird; light, tinny. I'd always wondered if I could keep my head if I found a body, and here I was, keeping my head, I told myself insanely as I watched him go down the hall to the pay phone. I was glad he didn't have to leave my sight. I might not be so level if I were standing in that hall alone, with a body behind me.

While Arthur muttered into the phone I kept my eyes on the door to the large room across the hall where John Queensland must be itching to open the meeting. I thought about what I'd just seen. I wasn't thinking about Mamie being dead, about the reality and finality of her death. I was thinking about the scene that had been staged, starring Mamie Wright as *the corpse*. The casting of the corpse had been deliberate, but the role of *the finder of the body* had by chance been taken by me. The whole thing was a scene deliberately staged by someone, and suddenly I knew what had been biting at me underneath the horror.

I thought faster than I'd ever thought before. I didn't feel sick anymore.

Arthur crossed the hall to the door of the large room and pushed it open just enough to insert his head in the gap. I could hear him address the other members of the club.

"Uh, folks, folks?" The voices stilled. "There's been an accident," he said with no emphasis. "I'm going to have to ask you all to stay in this room for a little while, until we can get things under control out here."

The situation, as far as I could see, was completely under control.

"Where's Roe Teagarden?" John Queensland's voice demanded.

Good old John. I'd have to tell Mother about that, she'd be touched.

"She's fine. I'll be back with you in a minute."

Gerald Wright's thin voice. "Where's my wife, Mr. Smith?"

"I'll get back with all of you in a few minutes," repeated the policeman firmly, and shut the door behind him. He stood lost in thought. I wondered if this detective had ever been the first on the scene of a murder investigation. He seemed to be ticking steps off mentally, from the way he was waggling his fingers and staring into space.

I waited. Then my legs started trembling and I thought I might fold again. "Arthur," I said sharply. "Detective Smith."

He jumped; he'd forgotten me. He took my arm solicitously.

I whacked at him with my free hand out of sheer aggravation. "I'm not trying to get you to help me, I want to tell you something!"

He steered me into a chair in the little conference room and put on a waiting face.

"I was supposed to lecture tonight on the Wallace case, you remember? William Herbert Wallace and his wife, Julia, England, 1931?"

He nodded his curly pale head and I could see he was a million miles away. I felt like slapping him again. I knew I sounded like an idiot, but I was coming to the point. "I don't know how much you remember about the Wallace case—if you don't know anything, I can fill you in later." I waved my hands to show that was inconsequential, here came the real meat. "What I want to tell you, what's important, is that Mamie Wright's been killed exactly like Julia Wallace. She's been *arranged*."

Bingo! That blue gaze was almost frighteningly intense now. I felt like a bug impaled on a pin. This was not a lightweight man.

"Point out a few comparisons before the lab guys get here, so I can have them photographed."

I blew out a breath of relief. "The raincoat under Mamie. It hasn't rained here in days. A raincoat was found under Julia Wallace. And Mamie's been placed by the little oven. Mrs. Wallace was found by a gas fire. She was bludgeoned to death. Like Mamie, I think. Mr. Wallace was an insurance salesman. So is Gerald Wright. I'll bet there's more I haven't thought of yet. Mamie's about the same age as Julia Wallace....There are just so many parallels I don't think I could've imagined them."

Arthur stared at me thoughtfully for a few long seconds. "Are there any photographs of the Wallace murder scene?" he asked.

The xeroxed pictures would have come in handy now, I thought.

"Yes, I've seen one, there may be more."

"Was the husband, Wallace, arrested?"

"Yes, and convicted. But later the sentence was overturned somehow or other, and he was freed."

"Okay. Come with me."

"One more thing," I said urgently. "The phone rang when I got here tonight and it was someone asking for Julia Wallace."

THREE

THE SILENT HALL WAS not silent anymore. As we left the conference room, the law came in the back door. It was represented by a heavy-set man in a plaid jacket who was taller and older than Arthur, and two men in uniform. As I stood back against the wall, temporarily forgotten, Arthur led them down the hall and opened the door to the kitchen. They crowded around the door looking in. They were all silent for a moment. The youngest man in uniform winced and then wrenched his face straight. The other uniformed man shook his head once and then stared in at Mamie with a disgusted expression. What disgusted him, I wondered? The mess that had been made with the body of a human being? The waste of a life? The fact that someone living in the town he had to protect had seen fit to do this terrible thing?

I realized the man in the plaid jacket was the sergeant of detectives; I'd seen his picture in the paper when he'd arrested a drug pusher. Now he pursed his mouth briefly and said "Damn," with little expression.

Arthur began telling them things, going swiftly and in a low voice. I could tell what point in his narrative he'd reached when their heads swung towards me simultaneously. I didn't know whether to nod or what. I just stared back at them and felt a thousand years old. Their faces turned back to Arthur and he continued his briefing.

The two men in uniform left the building while Arthur and the sergeant continued their discussion. Arthur seemed to be enumerating things, while the sergeant nodded his head in approval and occasionally interjected some comment. Arthur had a little notebook out and was jotting in it as they spoke.

Another memory about the sergeant stirred.

His name was Jack Burns. He'd bought his house from my mother. He was married to a school teacher and had two kids in college. Now Jack Burns gave Arthur a sharp nod, as clear as a starting gun. Arthur went to the door to the meeting room and pushed it open.

"Mr. Wright, could you come here for a minute, please?" Detective Arthur Smith asked, in a voice so devoid of expression that it was a warning in itself.

Gerald Wright came into the hall hesitantly. No one in the big room could fail to know by now that something was drastically wrong, and I wondered what they'd been saying. Gerald took a step toward me, but Arthur took his arm quite firmly and guided Gerald into the little conference room. I knew he was about to tell Gerald that his wife was dead, and I found myself wondering how Gerald would take it. Then I was ashamed.

At moments I understood in decent human terms what had happened to a woman I knew, and at moments I seemed to be thinking of Mamie's death as one of our club's study cases.

"Miss Teagarden," said Jack Burns's good-old-boy drawl, "you must be Aida Teagarden's child."

Well, I had a father, too: but he'd committed the dreadful sin of coming in from foreign parts (Texas) to work on our local Georgia paper, marrying my mother, begetting me, and then leaving and divorcing Lawrenceton's own Aida Brattle Teagarden. I said, "Yes."

"I'm mighty sorry you had to see something like that," Jack Burns said, shaking his heavy head mournfully.

It was almost like a burlesque of regret, it was laid on so heavily; was he being sarcastic? I looked down, and for once said nothing. I didn't need this right now; I was shaken and confused.

"It just seems so strange to me that a sweet young woman like you would come to a club like this," Jack Burns went on slowly, his tone expressing stunned bewilderment. "Could you just kind of clarify for me what the purpose of this—organization—is?"

I had to answer a direct question. But why was he asking me? His own detective belonged to the same club. I wished this middle-aged man with his plaid suit and his cowboy boots would melt through the floor. As slightly as I knew Arthur, I wanted him back. This man was scarey. I pushed my glasses back up my nose with shaking fingers.

"We meet once a month," I said in an uneven voice. "And we talk about a famous murder case, usually a pretty old one."

The sergeant apparently gave this deep thought. "Talk about it—?" he inquired gently.

"Ah...sometimes just learn about it, who was killed and how and why and by whom." Our members favored different "W's."

I was most interested in the victim.

"Or sometimes," I stumbled on, "depending on the case, we decide if the police arrested the right person. Or if the murder was unsolved, we talk about who may have been guilty. Sometimes we watch a movie."

"Movie?" Raised beetly brows, a gentle inquiring shake of the head.

"Like *The Thin Blue Line.* Or a fictionalized movie based on a real case. *In Cold Blood...*"

"But not ever," he asked delicately, "what you would call a—snuff movie?"

"Oh my God," I said sickly. "Oh my God, no." In my naivete, I said, "How could you think that?"

"Well, Miss Teagarden, this here is a real murder, and we have to ask real questions." And his face was not nice at all. Our club had offended something in Jack Burns. How would Arthur fare, a policeman who was actually a member? But it seemed he would be working on the investigation in some capacity.

"Now, Miss Teagarden," Jack Burns went on, his mask back in place, his voice as buttery as a waffle, "I am going to head up this investigation, and my two homicide detectives will work on this, and Arthur Smith will assist us, since he knows all you people. I know you'll cooperate to the fullest with him. He tells me you know a little more about this than the others, that you got some kind of phone call and you found the body. We may have to talk to you a few times about this, but you just have patience with us." And I knew from his face I had better be willing to turn over my every waking minute, if that was required of me.

By this time I felt that Arthur Smith was my oldest and dearest friend, so much safer did he seem than this terrifying man with his terrifying questions. And he stepped out from behind his sergeant now, his face blank and his eyes cautious. He'd heard at least some of this conversation, which would have sounded almost routine without Burns's menacing manner.

"Miss Teagarden," Arthur said brusquely, "will you go into the room with the others now? Please don't discuss with them what's happened out here. And thanks." With Gerald presumably grieving in the small conference room and Mamie dead in the

kitchen, I had to join the others unless he wanted me
to stand in the bathroom.

With a medley of feelings, relief predominating, I
was pushing open the door when I felt a hand on my
arm. "Sorry," murmured Arthur. Over his shoulder,
I saw the plaid back of Sergeant Burns's jacket as he
held open the back door to admit uniformed policemen loaded down with equipment. "If you don't
mind, I'll come to see you tomorrow morning about
this Wallace thing. Will you be at work?"

"Tomorrow's my day off," I said. "I can be at
home tomorrow morning."

"Nine o'clock too early?"

"No, that's fine."

As I went in the larger room where my fellow club
members were clustered anxiously, I thought about the
intelligence pitted against Arthur Smith's. Someone
was painstaking and artistic in a debased and imagi-
native way. Someone had issued a challenge to whoever cared to take it up. "Figure out who I am if you
can, you amateur students of crime. I've graduated to
the real thing. Here is my work."

I felt an instinctive urge to hide what I was thinking. I wiped my mind clean of my nasty thoughts and
tried not to meet the eyes of any of my fellow club
members, who were all waiting tensely for me in the
big room. But Sally Allison was a pro at catching reluctant eyes, and I saw her mouth open when she

caught mine. I knew beyond a doubt she was going to ask me if I'd found Mamie Wright. Sally was no fool. I shook my head firmly, and she came no closer.

"Are you all right, child?" John Queensland asked, advancing with the dignity that was the keystone of his character. "Your mother will be terribly upset when she hears . . ." but since John, who was after all a wee mite pompous, realized he had no idea what my mother was going to hear, he had to trail off into silence. He asked me a question with a look.

"I'm sorry," I said in a tiny squeak. I shook my head in irritation. "I'm sorry," I said more strongly, "I don't think Detective Smith wants me to talk until he talks to you." I gave John a small smile and went to sit by myself in a chair by the coffee urn, trying to ignore the indignant looks and mutters of dissatisfaction cast in my direction. Gifford Doakes was walking back and forth as if he were pacing a cage. The policemen outside seemed to be making him extremely nervous. The novelist Robin Crusoe was looking eager and curious; Lizanne just looked bored. LeMaster Cane, Melanie and Bankston, and Jane Engle were talking together in low voices. For the first time, I realized another club member, Benjamin Greer, was missing. Benjamin's attendance was erratic, like his life in general, so I didn't put any particular weight on that. Sally was sitting by her son Perry, whose thin slash of a mouth was twisted into a very peculiar smile. Perry's elevator did not stop at every floor.

I poured myself a cup of coffee, wishing it were a shot of bourbon. I thought of Mamie getting to the meeting early, setting everything up, making this very coffee so we wouldn't have to drink Sally's dreadful brew...I burst into tears, and slopped coffee all down my yellow sweater.

Those awful turquoise shoes. I kept seeing that empty shoe sitting upright in the middle of the floor.

I heard a soft sweet soothing murmur and knew Lizanne Buckley had come to my aid. Lizanne generously blocked me from the view of the room with an uncomfortable hunch of her tall body. I heard the scrape of a chair and saw a pair of long thin trousered legs. Her escort, the red-headed novelist, was helping her out, and then he tactfully moved away. Lizanne lowered herself into the chair and hitched it closer to me. Her manicured hand stuffed a handkerchief into my stubby one.

"Let's just think about something else," Lizanne said in a low even voice. She seemed quite sure I could think about something else. "Stupid ole me," said Lizanne charmingly. "I just can't get interested in the things this Robin Crusoe likes, like people getting murdered. So if you like him, you're welcome to him. I think maybe you and him would suit each other. Nothing wrong with him," she added hastily, in case

I should assume she was offering me something shoddy. "He'd just be happier with you, I think. Don't you?" she asked persuasively. She just knew a man would make me feel better.

"Lizanne," I said, with a few gasps and sobs interposed here and there, "you're wonderful. I don't know anyone to top you. There aren't too many single men our age in Lawrenceton to date, are there?"

Lizanne looked puzzled. She'd obviously noticed no lack of single men to date. I wondered where all her men came from. Probably drove from as far away as two hundred miles. "Thanks, Lizanne," I said helplessly.

Sergeant Burns appeared in the doorway and scanned the room. I had no doubt he was memorizing each and every face. I could tell by his scowl when he saw her that he knew Sally Allison was a reporter. He looked even angrier when he saw Gifford Doakes, who stopped his pacing and stared back at Burns with a sneering face.

"Okay, folks," he said peremptorily, eyeing us as if we were rather degenerate strangers caught half-dressed, "we've had a death here."

That could hardly have been a bombshell—after all, the people in this group were adept at picking up clues. But there was a shocked-sounding buzz of conversation in the wake of Burns's announcement. A few reactions were marked. Perry Allison got a strange smirk on his face, and I was even more strongly reminded that in the past Perry had had what people called "nervous problems," though he did his work at the library well enough. His mother Sally was watching his face with obvious anxiety. The red-haired writer's face lit with excitement, though he decently tried to tone it down. None of this could touch him personally, of course. He was new in town, had barely met a soul, and this was his first visit to Real Murders.

I envied him.

He saw me watching him, observing his excitement, and he turned red.

Burns said clearly, "I'm going to take you out of the room one by one, to the smaller room across the hall, and one of our uniformed officers will take your statement. Then I'm going to let you go home, though we'll need to talk to you all again later, I imagine. I'll start with Miss Teagarden, since she's had a shock."

Lizanne pressed my hand when I got up to leave. As I crossed the hall, I saw the building was teeming with police. I hadn't known Lawrenceton had that many in uniform. I was learning a lot tonight, one way or another.

The business of having my statement taken would have been interesting if I hadn't been so upset and tired. After all, I'd read about police procedure for years, about police questioning all available witnesses to a crime, and here I was, being questioned by a real policeman about a real crime. But the only lasting impression I carried away with me was that of thoroughness. Every question was asked twice, in different ways. The phone call, of course, came in for a great deal of attention. The pity of it was that I could say so little about it. I was faintly worried when Jack Burns stepped in and asked me very persistently about Sally Allison and her movements and demeanor; but I had to face the fact that since Sally and I were first on the scene (though we didn't know it at the time) we would be questioned most intensely.

I had my fingerprints taken, too, which would have been very interesting under other circumstances. As I left the room I glanced toward the kitchen without wanting to. Mamie Wright, housewife and wearer of high heels, was being processed as the *murder victim.* I didn't know where Gerald Wright was; since the small conference room had been free, he must have been driven home or even to the police station. Of course he would be the most suspected, and I knew chances were he'd probably done it, but I could find no relief in the thought.

I didn't believe Gerald had done it. I thought the person, man or woman, who'd called the VFW Hall had done it, and I didn't believe Gerald Wright would have resorted to such elaborate means if he'd wanted to kill Mamie. He might have buried her in his cellar, like Crippen, but he would not have killed her at the

VFW and then called to alert the rest of the club members to his actions. Actually, Gerald didn't seem to have enough sense of fun, if that was what you wanted to term it. This murder had a kind of bizarre playfulness about it. Mamie'd been arranged like a doll, and the phone call was like a childish "Nyah, nyah, you can't catch me."

As I went out to my car very slowly, I was mulling over that phone call. It was a red flag, surely, to alert the club to the near certainty that this murder had been planned and executed by a club member. Mamie Wright, wife of an insurance salesman in Lawrenceton, Georgia, had been battered to death and arranged after death to copy the murder of the wife of an insurance company employee in Liverpool, England. This had been done on the premises where the club met, on the night it met to discuss that very case. It was possible someone outside the club had a grudge against us, though I couldn't imagine why. No, someone had decided to have his own kind of fun with us. And that someone was almost surely someone I knew, almost surely a member of Real Murders.

I could scarcely believe I had to walk out to my car by myself, drive it home by myself, enter my dark home—by myself. But then I realized that all the members of Real Murders, alive or dead, with the exception of Benjamin Greer, were under police scrutiny at this very moment.

I was the safest person in Lawrenceton.

I drove slowly, double-checked myself at stop signs, and used my turn signals long before I needed to. I was so completely tired I was afraid I'd look drunk to any passing patrol officers . . . if there were any left on the streets. I was so glad to turn the car into my familiar slot, put my key in my own lock, and plod into my own territory. Functioning through a woolly fog of fatigue, I dialled Mother's number. When she answered I told her that no matter what she heard, I was just fine and nothing awful had happened to me. I cut off her questions, left the phone off the hook, and saw by the kitchen clock that it was only 9:30. Amazing.

I trudged up the stairs, pulling off my sweater and shirt as I went. I just managed to shuck the rest of my clothes, pull on my nightgown, and crawl into bed before sleep hit me.

At 3 A.M. I woke in a cold sweat. My dream had been one big close-up of Mamie Wright's head.

Someone was crazy; or someone was unbelievably vicious.

Or both.

FOUR

I TURNED THE WATER on full force, let it get good and hot, and stepped into the shower. It was 7 A.M. on a cool, crisp spring morning, and my first conscious thought was: I don't have to go to work today. The next thought was: my life has changed forever.

Not much had ever really happened to me; not big things, either wonderful or horrible. My parents getting divorced was bad, but even I had been able to see it was better for them. I had already gotten my driver's license by then, so they didn't need to shuttle me back and forth. Maybe the divorce had made me cautious, but caution is not a bad thing. I had a neat and tidy life in a messy world, and if sometimes I suspected I was trying to fulfill the stereotype of a small-town librarian, well, I had yearnings to play other roles, too. In the movies, sometimes those dry librarians with their hair in buns suddenly let their juices gush, shook their hair loose, threw off their glasses, and did a tango.

Maybe I would. But in the meantime, I could have a small pride in myself. I had done okay the night before, not great but okay. I had gotten through it.

I went through the tedious business of drying my mass of hair and pulled on some old jeans and a sweater. I padded downstairs in my moccasins and brewed some coffee, a big pot. I'd gotten my lawn chairs and table set up on the patio a week before, when I'd decided it was going to stay spring for good, so after getting my papers from the little-used front doorstep, I carried my first cup out to the patio. It was possible to feel alone there, though of course the Crandalls on one side and Robin Crusoe on the other could see my patio from their second floor back bedroom. The back bedroom was small and I knew everyone used it as a guest room, so the chances were good that no one was looking.

Sally hadn't managed to get the story in the local paper. I was sure that had been printed before the meeting even started. But the local man employed by the city paper had had better luck. "**Lawrenceton Woman Murdered**" ran the uninspired headline in the City and State section. A picture of Mamie accompanied the article, and I was impressed by the stringer's industry. I scanned the story quickly. It was necessarily short, and had little in it I didn't know, except that the police hadn't found Mamie's purse. I frowned at that. It didn't seem to fit somehow. There was no hint of this murder being like any other murder. I wondered if the police had requested that be withheld. But it would be all over Lawrenceton soon, I was sure.

Lawrenceton, despite its new population of commuters to Atlanta, was still a small town at heart. My name was included: *"Ms. Teagarden, anxious at Mrs. Wright's continued absence, searched the building and found Mrs. Wright's body in the kitchen."* I shivered. It sounded so simple in print.

I'd put the phone back on the hook, and now it rang. Mother, of course, I thought, and went back into the kitchen. I picked up the receiver as I poured more coffee.

"Are you all right?" she asked immediately. "John Queensland came over last night after the police let him go, and he told me all about it."

John Queensland was certainly making a determined effort to endear himself to Mother. Well, she'd been on her own (but not always alone) for a long time.

"I'm pretty much all right," I said cautiously.

"Was it awful?"

"Yes," I said, and I meant it. It had been horrible, but exciting, and the more hours separated me from the event, the more exciting and bearable it was becoming. I didn't want to lose the horror; that was what kept you civilized.

"I'm sorry," she said helplessly. Neither of us knew what to say next. "Your father called me," she blurted out. "You must have had your phone off the hook?"

"Uh-huh."

"He was worried, too. About you. And he said you were going to keep Phillip next weekend? He wondered if you would be able; he said if you didn't feel like it, just give him a call, he'd change his plans." Mother was doing her best not to call her ex-husband a selfish bastard for mentioning such a thing at a time like this.

I had a half-brother, Phillip, six, a scarey and wonderful boy whom I could stand for whole weekends occasionally without my nerves completely shattering. I'd completely forgotten that Dad and his second wife Betty Jo (quite a reaction to an Aida Teagarden) were leaving for a convention in Chattanooga in a few days.

"No, that'll be okay, I'll give him a call later today," I said.

"Well. You will call me if you need me to do anything? I can bring you some lunch, or you can come stay with me."

"No, I'm fine." A slight exaggeration, but close enough to the truth. I suddenly wanted to say something real, something indelible, to my mother. But the only thing I could think of wouldn't bear uttering. I wanted to say I felt more alive than I had in years; that finally something bigger than myself had happened to me. Now, instead of reading about an old murder, seeing passion and desperation and evil in print on a page, I knew these things to be possessed by people around me. And I said, "Really, I'm okay. And the police are coming by this morning; I'd better go get ready."

"All right, Aurora. But call me if you get scared. And you can always stay here."

I had a sudden flood of nervous energy after I hung up. I looked around me, and decided to put it to good use picking up. First my den/dining room/kitchen right off the patio, then the formal front room that I seldom used. I checked the little downstairs bathroom for toilet paper, and ran up the stairs to make my bed and straighten up. The guest bedroom was pristine, as usual. I gathered up my dirty clothes and trotted downstairs with the bundle, tossing it unceremoniously down the basement stairs to land in front of the washer. Lawrenceton is on high enough ground for basements to be feasible.

When I looked at the clock and saw I had fifteen minutes left before Arthur Smith was due to come, I checked the coffee level and went back upstairs to put on some makeup. That was simple enough, since I wore little, and I hardly had to look in the mirror to do it. But out of habit I did, and I didn't look any more interesting or experienced than I had the day before. My face was still pale and round, my nose short and straight and suitable for holding up my glasses, my eyes magnified behind those glasses and round and brown. My hair unbound flew all around my head in a waving brown mass halfway down my back, and for once I let it be. It would get in my way and stick to the corners of my mouth and get caught in the hinges of my glasses, but what the hell! Then I heard the double ring of the front doorbell and flew downstairs.

People almost always came to the back door instead of the front, but Arthur had parked on the street instead of in the parking area behind the apartments. Under the fresh suit, shaved jaw, and curling pale hair still damp from the shower, he looked tired.

"Are you all right this morning?" he asked.

"Yes, pretty much. Come in."

He looked all around him, openly, when he passed through the living room, missing nothing. He paused at the big room where I really lived. "Nice," he said, sounding impressed. The sunny room with the big window overlooking the patio with its rose trees did look attractive. Exposed brick walls and all the books make an intelligent-looking room, anyway, I thought, and I waved him onto the tan suede love seat as I asked him if he wanted coffee.

"Yes, black," he said fervently. "I was up most of the night."

When I bent over to put his cup on the low table in front of him, I realized with some embarrassment that his eyes weren't on the coffee cup.

I settled opposite him in my favorite chair, low enough that my feet can touch the floor, wide enough to curl up inside, with a little table beside it just big enough to hold a book and a coffee cup.

Arthur took a sip of his coffee, eyed me again as he told me it was good, and got down to business.

"You were right, the body was definitely moved after death to the position it was in when you found it," he said directly. "She was killed there in the kitchen. Jack Burns is having a hard time swallowing this theory, that she was deliberately killed to mimic the Wallace murder, but I'm going to try to convince him. He's in charge though; I'm assisting on this one since I know all the people involved, but I'm really a burglary detective."

Some questions flew through my head, but I decided it wouldn't be polite to ask them. Sort of like asking a doctor about your own symptoms at a party. "Why is Jack Burns so scarey?" I asked abruptly. "Why does he make an effort to intimidate you? What's the point?"

At least Arthur didn't have to ask me what I meant. He knew exactly what Jack Burns was like.

"Jack doesn't care if people like him or not," Arthur said simply. "That's a big advantage, especially to a cop. He doesn't even care if other cops like him. He just wants cases solved as soon as possible, he wants witnesses to tell him everything they know, and he wants the guilty punished. He wants the world to go his way, and he doesn't care what he has to do to make it happen.''

That sounded pretty frightening to me. "At least you know where you are with him," I said weakly. Arthur nodded matter-of-factly.

"Tell me everything you know about the Wallace case," he said.

"Well, I'm up on it of course, since it was supposed to be the topic last night," I explained. "I wonder if—whoever killed Mamie—picked it for that reason?"

I was actually kind of glad I'd finally get to deliver part of my laboriously prepared lecture. And to a fellow aficionado, a professional at that.

"The ultimate murder mystery, according to several eminent crime writers," I began. "William Herbert Wallace, Liverpool insurance salesman," I raised a finger to indicate one point of similarity, "and married with no children," I raised a second finger. Then I thought Arthur could probably do without me telling him his job. "Wallace and his wife Julia were middle aged and hadn't much money, but did have intellectual leanings. They played duets together in the evening. They didn't entertain much or have many friends. They weren't known to quarrel.

"Wallace had a regular schedule for collecting insurance payments from subscribers to his particular company, and he'd bring the money home with him for one night, Tuesday. Wallace played chess, too, and was entered in a tournament at a local club. There was a play off chart establishing when he'd be playing, posted on the wall at the club. Anyone who came in could see it." I raised my eyebrows at Arthur to make sure he marked that important point. He nodded.

"Okay. Wallace didn't have a phone at home. He got a call at the chess club right before he arrived there one day. Another member took the message. The caller identified himself as 'Qualtrough.' The caller said that he wanted to take out a policy on his daughter and asked that Wallace be given a message to come around to Qualtrough's house the next evening, Tuesday.

"Now, the bad thing about this call, from Wallace's point of view," I explained, warming to my subject, "is that it came to the club when Wallace wasn't there. And there was a telephone booth Wallace could have used, close to his home, if he himself placed the 'Qualtrough' call."

Arthur scribbled in a little leather notepad he produced from somewhere.

"Now—Wallace comes in very soon after Qualtrough has called the club. Wallace talks about this message to the other chess players. Maybe he means to impress it on their memory? Either he is a murderer and is setting up his alibi, or the real murderer is making sure Wallace will be out of the house Tuesday evening. And this dual possibility, that almost hanged Wallace, runs throughout the case." Could any writer have imagined anything as interesting as this? I wanted to ask.

But instead I plunged back in. "So on the appointed night Wallace goes looking for this man Qualtrough who wants to take out some insurance. Granted, he was a man who needed all the business he could get, and granted, we know what insurance salesmen are still like today, but even so Wallace went to extreme lengths to find this potential customer. The address Qualtrough left at the chess club was in Menlove Gardens East. There's a Menlove Gardens North, South and West, but no Menlove Gardens East; so it was a clever false address to give. Wallace asks many people he meets—even a policeman!—if they know where he can find this address. He may be stubborn, or he may be determined to fix himself in the memories of as many people as possible.

"Since there simply was no such address, he went home."

I paused to take a long drink of my tepid coffee.

"She was already dead?" Arthur asked astutely.

"Right, that's the point. If Wallace killed her, he had to have done it before he left on this wild goose chase. If so, what I'm about to tell you was all acting.

"He gets home and tried to open his front door, he later says. His key won't work. He thinks Julia has bolted the front door and for some reason can't hear him knock. Whatever was the case, a couple who live next door leave their house and see Wallace at his back door, apparently in distress. He tells them about the front door being bolted. Either his distress is genuine, or he's been hanging around in the back alley waiting for someone else to witness his entrance.''

Arthur's blond head shook slowly from side to side as he contemplated the twists and turns of this classic. I imagined the Liverpool police force in 1931 sitting and shaking their heads in exactly the same way. Or perhaps not; they'd been convinced early on that they had their man.

"Was Wallace friendly with those neighbors?" he asked.

"Not particularly. Good, but impersonal, relationship."

"So he could count on their being accepted as impartial witnesses," Arthur observed.

"If he did it. Incidentally, the upshot of all this about the front door lock, which Wallace said resisted his key, turned out to be a major point in the trial, but the testimony was pretty murky. Also iffy was the evidence of a child who knocked on the door with the day's milk, or a newspaper or something. Mrs. Wallace answered the door, alive and well; and if it could have been proved Wallace had already left, he would have been cleared. But it couldn't be." I took a deep breath. Here came the crucial scene. "Be that as it may. Wallace and the couple *do* enter the house, *do* see a few things out of place in the kitchen and another room, I think, but no major ransacking. The box where Wallace kept the insurance money had been rifled. Of course, this was a Tuesday, when there should've been a lot of money.

"The neighbors by this time are scared. Then Wallace calls them into the front room, a parlor, rarely used.

"Julia Wallace is there, lying in front of the gas fire, with a raincoat under her. The raincoat, partially burned, is not hers. She's been beaten to death, with extreme brutality, unnecessary force. She has not been raped." I stopped suddenly. "I assume Mamie wasn't?" I said finally, frightened of the answer.

"Doesn't look like it right now," Arthur said absently, still taking notes.

I blew my breath out. "Well, Wallace theorizes that 'Qualtrough,' who of course must be the murderer if Wallace is innocent, called at the house after Wallace left. He was evidently someone Julia didn't know well, or at all, because she showed him into the company parlor." Just like I would an insurance salesman, I thought. "The raincoat, an old one of Wallace's, she perhaps threw over her shoulders because the disused room was cold until the gas fire, which she apparently lit, had had a chance to heat it. The money that had been taken hadn't actually been much, since Wallace had been ill that week and hadn't been able to collect everything he was supposed to. But no one else would have known that, presumably.

"Julia certainly hadn't been having an affair, and had never personally offended anyone that the police could discover.

"And that's the Wallace case."

Arthur sat lost in thought, his blue eyes fixed intently on some internal point. "Wobbly, either way," he said finally.

"Right," I agreed. "There's no real case against Wallace, except that he was her husband, the only person who seemed to know her well enough to kill her. Everything he said could've been true...in which case, he was tried for killing the one person in the world he loved, while all the time the real killer went free."

"So Wallace was arrested?"

"And convicted. But after he spent some time in prison, he was released by a unique ruling in British law. I think a higher court simply ruled that there hadn't been enough evidence for a jury to convict Wallace, no matter what the jury said. But prison and the whole experience had broken Wallace, and he died two or three years later, still saying he was innocent. He said he suspected who Qualtrough was, but he had no proof."

"I'd have gone for Wallace, too, on the basis of that evidence," Arthur said unhesitatingly. "The probability is with Wallace, as you said, because it's usually the husband who wants his wife out of the way...yet since there's no clearcut evidence either way, I'm almost surprised the state chose to prosecute."

"Probably," I said without thinking, "the police were under a lot of pressure to make an arrest."

Arthur looked so tired and gloomy that I tried to change the subject. "Why'd you join Real Murders?" I asked. "Isn't that a little strange for a policeman?"

"Not this policeman," he said a little sharply. I shrank in my chair.

"Listen, Roe, I wanted to go to law school, but there wasn't enough money." Arthur's family was pretty humble, I recalled. I thought I'd gone to high school with one of his sisters. Arthur must be three or four years older than I. "I made it through two years of college before I realized I couldn't make it financially, because I just couldn't work and carry a full course load. School bored me then, too. So I decided to go into law from another angle. Policemen aren't all alike, you know."

I could tell he'd given this lecture before.

"Some cops are right out of Joseph Wambaugh's books, because he was a cop and he writes pretty good books. Loud, drinkers, macho, mostly uneducated, sometimes brutal. There are a few nuts, like there are in any line of work, and there are a few Birchers. There aren't many Liberals with a capital 'L', and not too many college graduates. But within those rough lines, we've got all kinds of people. Some of my friends—some cops—watch every cop show on television they can catch, so they'll know how to act. Some of them—not many—read Dostoevsky." He smiled, and it looked almost strange on him. "I just like to study old crimes, figure out how the police thought on the case, pick apart their procedure—ever read about the June Anne Devaney case, Blackburn, England, oh, about late 1930's?"

"A child murder, right?"

"Right. You know the police persuaded every adult male in Blackburn to have his fingerprints taken?" Arthur's face practically shone with enthusiasm. "That's how they caught Peter Griffiths. By comparing thousands of fingerprints with the ones Griffiths left on the scene." He was lost in admiration for a moment. "That's why I joined Real Murders," he said. "But what could a woman like Mamie Wright get out of studying the Wallace case?"

"Oh, a chaperoned husband!" I said with a grin, and then felt a sharp pang of dismay as Arthur reopened his little notebook.

Almost gently, Arthur said, "Now, this murder is real. It's a new murder."

"I know," I said, and I saw Mamie again.

"Did they quarrel much, Gerald and Mamie?"

"Never, that I saw or heard," I said firmly and truthfully. I'd always believed Wallace was innocent. "She just seemed to be keeping an eye on him around other women."

"Do you think her suspicions were correct?"

"It never occurred to me they could be. Gerald is just so stuffy and...Arthur? Could Gerald have done this?" I didn't mean emotionally, I meant practically, and Arthur realized it.

"Do you know why Gerald says he was late to the meeting, why Mamie came on her own instead of riding with him? He got a call from a man he didn't know, asking Gerald to talk with him about some insurance for his daughter."

I know my mouth was hanging open. I slowly shut it, but feared I looked no more intelligent.

"Someone's really slapping us in the face, Arthur," I said slowly. "Maybe especially challenging you. Mamie wasn't even killed because she was *Mamie*." That was especially horrible. "It was just because she was an insurance salesman's wife."

"But you'd figured it out last night. You know that."

"But what if there are more? What if he copies the June Anne Devaney murder, and kills a three-year-old? What if he copies the Ripper murders? Or kills people like Ed Gein did, to eat?''

"Don't go imagining nightmares," Arthur said briskly. He was so matter of fact I knew he'd already thought of the possibility himself. "Now, I've got to write down everything you did yesterday, starting from when you left work."

If he meant to jolt me out of the horrors, he succeeded. Even if only on paper, I was someone who had to account for her movements; not exactly a suspect, but a possibility. Then too, my arrival time at the meeting would help pinpoint the time of death. Though I'd gone over this all the night before, once more I carefully related my trivial doings.

"Do you have a good account of the Wallace killing I could borrow?" he asked, rising from the couch reluctantly. He looked even more worn, as if relaxing for a while hadn't helped, just made him feel his exhaustion. "And I need a list of club members, too."

"I can help you with the Wallace killing," I said. "But you'll have to get the list from Jane Engle. She's the club secretary." I had the book on hand I'd used to prepare my lecture. I checked to make sure my name was written inside, told Arthur I'd have him arrested if he didn't return it, and walked with him to the front door.

To my surprise, he put his hands on my shoulders and gripped them with no mean pressure.

"Don't look so dismal," he said. The wide blue eyes caught mine. I felt a jolt tingle up my spine. "You caught something last night most people wouldn't have. You were tough and smart and quick-thinking." He caught a loose strand of my hair and rolled it between his fingers. "I'll talk to you soon," he said. "Maybe tomorrow."

As it turned out, we spoke somewhat sooner than that.

FIVE

I'D NOTICED A MOVING van parked in front of Robin Crusoe's apartment when I let Arthur out. Out of sheer curiosity, when the phone began to ring, I decided to take my calls on my bedside phone, which had a long cord, so I could stare out the front windows at the unloading. And the phone was ringing non-stop, as the news about Mamie Wright's murder spread among friends and co-workers. Just when I was about to dial his number, my father called. He seemed about equally concerned with my emotional health and with whether or not I still felt I could keep Phillip.

"Are you okay?" Phillip himself said softly. He is a shrieker in person, but unaccountably soft-spoken over the telephone.

"Yes, brother, I'm okay," I answered.

"'Cause I really want to come see you. Can I?"

"Sure."

"Are you going to make pecan pie?"

"I might, if I was asked nicely."

"Please, please, please?"

"That's pretty nice. Count on the pie."

"Yahoo!"

"Do you feel I'm blackmailing you?" Father asked when Phillip relinquished the phone.

"Well, yes."

"Okay, okay, I feel guilty. But Betty Jo really wants to go to this convention. Her best friend from college married a newspaperman, too, and they're going to be there."

"Tell her I'll still keep him." I loved Phillip, though at first I'd been terrified to even hold him, having no experience whatsoever with babies. To give Betty Jo credit, she's always been all for Phillip's getting to know his big sister.

After I'd hung up, the rest of the day gaped ahead of me like a black cave. Since it was my day off I tried to do day-off things; I paid bills, did my laundry.

My best friend, Amina Day, had just moved to Houston to take such a good job that I couldn't grudge her the move; but I missed her, and I'd felt very much an unadventurous village bumpkin before I'd stepped into the VFW kitchen. Amina wasn't going to believe I'd had a bona fide shocking experience right in Lawrenceton. I decided to call her that night, and the prospect cheered me.

Now that the first shock of last night had worn off, it all seemed curiously unreal, like a book. I'd read so many books, both fiction and nonfiction, in which a young woman walked into a room (across a field, down the stairs, in an alley) and found *the body*. I could distance myself from the reality of a dead Mamie by thinking of the situation, rather than the person.

I picked out all these distinctions while eating a nutritious lunch of Cheezits and tuna fish. All this thinking led me back to the depressing conclusion that so little had happened in my life for so long, that when something did I had to pick at it over and over. No moment was going to sneak by *me* unobserved and unanalyzed.

Clearly, some action was called for.

With the taste of lunch in my mouth it was easy to decide that that action should take the form of going to the grocery store. I made one of my methodical little lists and gathered up my coupons.

Of course the store was extra crowded on Saturday, and I saw several people who knew what had happened the night before. I found myself reluctant to talk about it to people who hadn't been there. I hadn't been asked to avoid mentioning the murder's connection to an old murder case, but I didn't see any sense in having to explain it to ten people in a row, either. Even the minimal responses I made slowed me down considerably, and forty minutes later I was only halfway through my list. As I stood at the meat counter debating between "lean" and "extra lean" hamburger, I heard a tapping noise. It grew more and more imperative, until I looked up. Benjamin Greer, the only member of Real Murders who hadn't been at the meeting the night before, was tapping on the clear glass that separated the butchers from the refrigerated meat counter. Behind him, gleaming steel machines were doing their job, and another butcher in a bloodstained apron like Benjamin's was packing roasts.

Benjamin was stout with wispy blond hair that he swept up and over his premature bald spot. He'd tried to grow a mustache to augment his missing scalp hair, but it had given the impression that his upper lip was dirty, and I was glad to see he'd shaved the thing off. He wasn't very tall, and he wasn't very bright, and he tried to make up for these factors with a puppylike friendliness and willingness to do whatever one asked. On the down side, if his help was not needed, no matter how tactfully you expressed it, he turned sullen and self-pitying. Benjamin was a difficult person, one of those people who make you feel ashamed of yourself if you dislike him, while making it almost impossible to like him.

I disliked him, of course. He'd asked me out three times, and every time, feeling deeply ashamed of myself, I'd told him no. Even as desperate for a date as I was, I couldn't stomach the thought of going out with Benjamin.

He'd tried a fundamentalist church, he'd tried coaching Little League, and now he was trying Real Murders.

I smiled at him falsely and damned the hamburger meat that had led me into his sight.

He hurried through the swinging door to the right of the meat. I steeled myself to be nice.

"The police came to my apartment last night," he said breathlessly. "They wanted to know why I hadn't come to the meeting."

"What did you say?" I asked bluntly. The blood-stained apron was making me feel unwell. Suddenly hamburger seemed quite distasteful.

"Oh, I hated to miss your presentation," he assured me, as if I'd been worried, "but I had something else I had to do." Put that in your pipe and smoke it, his expression said. Benjamin's words were as mild and apologetic and his voice was as abased as usual, but his face was another matter.

I looked inquiring and waited. Definitely not the hamburger. Maybe no red meat at all.

"I'm in politics," Benjamin told me, his voice modest but his face triumphant.

"The mayoral race?" I guessed.

"Right. I'm helping out Morrison Pettigrue. I'm his campaign manager." And Benjamin's voice quivered with pride.

Whoever Morrison Pettigrue was, he was sure to lose. The name rang a faint bell, but I wasn't willing to stand there waiting to recall what I knew.

"I wish you luck," I said with as good a smile as I could scrape together.

"Would you like to go to a rally with me next week?"

My God, he *wanted* me to kick him in the face. That was the only explanation. I looked at him and thought, you pathetic person. Then I felt ashamed, of course, and that made me angry at myself, and him.

"No, Benjamin," I said with finality. I could not offer an excuse. I did not want this to happen again.

"Okay," he said, with martyrdom in his voice. "Well . . . I'll be seeing you." The hurt quivered dramatically just under his brave smile.

The old reply came to the tip of my tongue, and I bit it back. But as I wheeled my cart away, I whispered, "Not if I see you first." As I slowed down to stare at the dog food bags, just so he wouldn't look out the window and see me speeding away as fast as I could move, I realized there were a couple of funny things about our conversation.

He hadn't asked any questions about last night. He hadn't asked who had been at the meeting, he hadn't said how strange it was that the only night he'd missed was the night something extraordinary happened. He hadn't even asked how it felt to discover Mamie's body, something everyone I'd seen today had been trying to ask me in roundabout ways.

I puzzled over it while I selected shampoo, and then decided not to worry about Benjamin Greer. Instead, I would get mad at the shelf stockers. Naturally, every kind of heavily sugared cereal based on a cartoon show was at my eye level, while cereal bought by grown-ups was stacked way above my head. I could reach them, but then the stockers had laid other boxes down on top of the row of upright boxes. If I pulled out the one I could reach, the others on top of it would come toppling down, making lots of noise and attracting lots of attention. You can tell I know from experience.

I turned sideways to maximize my stretch and stood on my tiptoes. No go. I was just going to have to switch brands or start eating cereal that tasted like bubble gum. That horrible thought galvanized me into another attempt.

"Here, young lady, let me get that for you," said an unbearably patronizing voice from somewhere above me. A huge hand reached over my head, grasped the box easily, and like a crane lowered the box into my cart.

I gripped the cart handle as if it were my temper. I breathed out once deeply, and then in again. I slowly turned to face my benefactor. I looked up—and up—into a comically dismayed face topped by a thatch of longish red hair.

"Oh, gosh, I'm sorry," said Robin Crusoe. Hazel eyes blinked at me anxiously from behind his wire-rims. "I thought—from the back, you know, you look about twelve. But certainly not from the *front*."

He realized what he'd just said, and his eyes closed in horror.

I was beginning to enjoy this.

A fleeting image crossed my mind of us in an intimate situation, and I wondered if it would work at all. I couldn't help it; I began to smile.

He smiled back, relieved, and I saw his charm instantly. He had a crooked smile, a little shy.

"I don't think we should talk like this," he said, indicating the difference in our heights. "Why don't I come over after I get my groceries put up? You live right by me, I think you said last night? You make me want to pick you up so I can see you better."

That so closely matched a certain image crossing my mind that I could feel my face turning red. "Please do come over. I'm sure you have a lot of questions after last night," I said.

"That would be great. My place is in such a mess that I need a break from looking at boxes."

"Okay, then. About an hour?"

"Sure, see you then—your name's really Roe?"

"Short for Aurora," I explained. "Aurora Teagarden."

He didn't seem to think my name was unusual at all.

"Coffee? Soft drink? Orange juice?" I offered.

"Beer?" he countered.

"Wine."

"Okay. I don't usually drink at this hour, but if anything will drive you to drink, it's moving."

Feeling naughty at having a drink before five in the afternoon, I filled two glasses and joined him in the living room. I sat in the same chair I'd taken that morning when Arthur had been there, and felt incredibly female and powerful at entertaining two men in my home on the same day.

Robin, like Arthur, was impressed with the room. "I hope mine looks half this good when I've finished unpacking. I have no talent at all for making things look nice."

My friend Amina would have said I didn't either. "Are you settled in?" I asked politely.

"I got my bed put together while the moving men were unloading the rest of the van, and I've hung my clothes in the closet. At least I had a chair for the detective to sit in this morning. They carried it in right as he walked to the door."

"Arthur Smith?" I was surprised. He hadn't told me he was going to interview Robin after he left my place. I'd shut the door assuming he'd get in his car and drive off. He must have left Robin's apartment before I started spying out the front upstairs window.

"Yes, he was checking up on the way I happened to come to the club meeting—"

"How *did* you know about it?" I interrupted with intense curiosity.

"Well," he said with reddening face, "when I went to the utility company, I got to talking with Lizanne, and when she found out I write mysteries, she remembered the club. Evidently you told her about it one time." I hadn't imagined Lizanne was listening. She'd looked, as usual, bored. "So Lizanne called John Queensland, who said Real Murders was meeting that very night and visitors could come, so I asked her..."

"Just wondered," I said neutrally.

"That Sergeant Burns, he's a grim kind of man," Robin said thoughtfully. "And Detective Smith is no lightweight."

"You didn't even know Mamie, it's out of the question you could be suspected."

"Well, I guess I could have known her before. But I didn't, and I think Smith believes that. But I bet he'll check. That's a guy I wouldn't like to have on my trail."

"Mamie wouldn't have gotten there before 7:00," I said thoughtfully. "And I have no alibi for 7:00 to 7:30. She had to meet the VFW president at the VFW Hall to get the key. And I think after every meeting she had to run by his house to return the key."

"Nope. Yesterday she dropped by the president's house and picked up the key. She told them she needed to get in early, she had some kind of appointment to meet someone there before the meeting."

"How'd you know that?" I was agog and indignant.

"The detective asked to use the phone to call the station and I pieced that together from listening to his end of the conversation," he said frankly. Aha, another person who was curious by nature.

"Oh. So," I said slowly, thinking as I went, "whoever killed her actually had plenty of time to fix everything up. He got her to come early somehow, so he'd have buckets of time to kill her and arrange her and go home to clean up." I drained my glass and shuddered.

Robin said hastily, "Tell me about the other club members."

I decided that question was the real purpose of his visit. I felt disappointed, but philosophical.

"Jane Engle, the white-haired older lady," I began. "She's retired but works from time to time substitute teaching or substituting at the library. She's an expert on Victorian murders." And then I ran down the list on my fingers: Gifford Doakes, Melanie Clark, Bankston Waites, John Queensland, LeMaster Cane, Arthur Smith, Mamie and Gerald Wright, Perry Allison, Sally Allison, Benjamin Greer. "But Perry's only just started coming," I explained. "I guess he's not really a member."

Robin nodded, and his red hair fell across his eyes. He brushed it back absently.

That absorption in his face and the small gesture did something to me.

"What about you?" he asked. "Give me a little biography."

"Not much to tell. I went to high school here, went to a small private college, did some graduate work at the university in library science and came home and got a job at the local library."

Robin looked disconcerted.

"All right, it never occurred to me not to come back," I said after a moment. "What about you?"

"Oh, I'm going to teach a course at the university. The writer they had lined up had a heart attack... Do you ever do impulsive things?" Robin asked suddenly.

One of the strongest impulses I'd ever felt urged me to put down my wine glass, walk over to Robin Crusoe, a writer I'd known only a few hours, sit on his lap, and kiss him until he fainted.

"Almost never," I said with real regret. "Why?"

"Have you ever experienced ..."

My doorbell chimed twice.

"Excuse me," I said with even deeper regret, and answered the front door.

Mr. Windham, my mail carrier, handed me a brown-wrapped package. "I couldn't fit this in your box," he explained.

I glanced at the mailing label. "Oh, it's not to me, it's to Mother," I said, puzzled.

"Well, we have to deliver by addresses, so I had to bring it here," Mr. Windham said righteously.

Of course, he was right; my address was on the package. The return address was my father's home in the city. The label itself was typed, as usual for Father. He's gotten a new typewriter, I thought, surprised. His old Smith-Corona had been the only typewriter he'd ever used. Maybe he'd mailed it to Mother from his office and used a typewriter there? Then I noticed the date.

"Six days?" I said incredulously. "It took six days for this to travel thirty miles?"

Mr. Windham shrugged defensively.

My father hadn't said a word about mailing us anything. As I shut the front door, I reflected that Father hadn't sent Mother a package in my memory, certainly never since the divorce. I was eaten up with curiosity. I stopped at the kitchen phone on my way back out to the patio. She was in her office, and said she'd stop by on her way to show a house. She was as puzzled as I was, and I hated to hear that little thread of excitement in her voice.

Robin seemed to be dozing in his chair, so I quietly picked up our wine glasses and washed them so I could put them away before Mother got there. I didn't need her arching her eyebrows at me. Actually, I was glad to have a breather. I'd almost done something radical earlier, and it was almost as much fun to think about nearly having done it as it would have been (maybe) to do it.

When Mother came through the gate, Robin woke up—if he'd really been asleep—and I introduced them.

Robin stood courteously, shook hands properly, and admired Mother as she was used to being admired, from her perfectly frosted hair to her slim elegant legs. Mother was wearing one of her very expensive suits, this one in a champagne color, and she looked like a million-dollar saleswoman. Which she was, several times over.

"So nice to see you again, Mr. Crusoe," she said in her husky voice. "I'm sorry you had such a bad experience your first evening in our little town. Really, Lawrenceton is a lovely place, and I'm sure you won't regret living here and commuting to the city."

I handed her the box. She looked at the return address sharply, then began ripping open the wrapping while she kept up an idle conversation with Robin.

"Mrs. See's!" we exclaimed simultaneously when we saw the white and black box.

"Candy?" Robin said uncertainly. He sat back down when I did.

"Very good candy," Mother said happily. "They sell it out west, and in the midwest too, but you can't get it down here. I used to have a cousin in St. Louis who'd send me a box every Christmas, but she passed away last year. So Roe and I were thinking we'd never get a box of Mrs. See's again!"

"I want the chocolate-almond clusters!" I reminded her.

"They're yours," Mother assured me. "You know I only like the creams . . . hum. No note. That's odd."

"I guess Dad just remembered how much you liked them," I offered, but it was a weak offering. Somehow the gesture just wasn't like my father; it was an impulse gift, since Mother's birthday was months away, and he hadn't been giving her a birthday present since they divorced, anyway. So, a nice impulse. But my father never did impulsive things; I came by my caution honestly.

Mother had offered the box to Robin, who shook his head. She settled down to the delightful task of choosing her first piece of Mrs. See's. It was one of our favorite little Christmas rituals, and the spring weather felt all wrong suddenly.

"It's been so long," she mused. She finally sighed and lifted a piece. "Aurora, isn't this the one with caramel filling?"

I peered at the chocolate in question. I was sitting down, Mother was standing up, so I could see what she hadn't. There was a hole in the bottom of the chocolate.

It had gotten banged around in shipment?

Abruptly I leaned forward and pulled another chocolate out of its paper frill. It was a nut cluster and it was pristine. I breathed out a sigh of relief. Just in case, I picked up another cream. It had a hole in the bottom, too.

"Mom. Put the candy down."

"Is this a piece you wanted?" she asked, eyebrows raised at my tone.

"Put it *down*."

She did, and looked at me angrily.

"There's something wrong with it, Mom. Robin, look." I poked at the piece she'd relinquished with my finger.

Robin lifted the chocolate delicately with his long fingers and peered at the bottom. He put it down and looked at several more. My mother looked cross and frightened.

"Surely this is ridiculous," she said.

"I don't think so, Mrs. Teagarden," Robin answered finally. "I think someone's tried to poison you, and maybe Roe too."

SIX

So ARTHUR CAME TO my apartment on official business twice in one day, and he brought another detective with him this time, or maybe she brought him. Lynn Liggett was a homicide detective, and she was as tall as Arthur, which made her tall for a woman.

I can't say I was afraid right then. I was confused at the label apparently addressed by my father, I was indignant that someone had tried to trick us into eating something unhealthy, but I was sure that with poisons being so hard to obtain, whatever was in the candy would prove to be something that might have caused us to have a few bad hours, but simply couldn't have killed Mother or me.

Arthur seemed pretty grim about the whole thing, and Lynn Liggett asked us questions. And more questions. I could see the lapel pin on Mother's jacket heave. When Detective Liggett bagged the candy and carried it out to Arthur's car, Mother said to me in a furious whisper, "She acts like we are people who don't live decent lives!"

"She doesn't know us, Mother," I said soothingly, though to tell the truth I was a little peeved with Detective Liggett myself. Questions like, "Have you recently finished a relationship that left someone bitter with you, Mrs. Teagarden?'' and ''Miss Teagarden, how long have you known Mr. Crusoe?'' had not left a good taste in my mouth either. I'd never before been able to understand why good citizens didn't cooperate with the police—after all, they had their job to do, they didn't know you personally, to them all citizens should be treated alike, blah blah blah, right?

Now I could understand. Jack Burns looking at me like I was a day-old catfish corpse had been one thing, an isolated incident maybe. I wanted to say, Liggett, romantic relationships don't figure in this, some maniac mailed this candy to Mother and dragged me into it by addressing it to me! But I knew Lynn Liggett was obliged to ask us these questions and I was bound to answer them. And still I resented it.

Maybe it wouldn't have bothered me if Lynn Liggett hadn't been a woman.

Not that I didn't think women should be detectives. I certainly did think women should be detectives, and I thought many women I knew would be great detectives—you should see some of my fellow librarians tracking down an overdue book, and I'm not being facetious.

But Lynn Liggett seemed to be evaluating me as a fellow woman, and she found me wanting. She looked down at me and found me smaller than her ''every whichaways,'' as I remembered my grandmother saying. I conjectured that since being tall must have given Detective Liggett problems, she automatically assumed I felt superior to her as a woman, since I was so short and therefore more "feminine." Since she couldn't compete with me on that level, Liggett figured she'd be tougher, more suspicious, coldly professional. A strong frontier woman as opposed to me, the namby-pamby useless stay-back-in-the-effete-east toy woman.

I know a lot about role-playing, and she couldn't pull that bull on me. I was tempted to burst into tears, pull out a lace handkerchief—if I had possessed such a useless thing—and say, "Ar-thur! Little ole me is just so scared!" Because I could see that this had little to do with me, but much to do with Arthur.

Getting right down to the nitty-gritty, Homicide Detective Liggett had the hots for Burglary Detective Smith, and as Detective Liggett saw it, Detective Smith had the hots for me.

It's taken me a long time to spell out what I sensed in a matter of minutes. I was disappointed in Lynn Liggett, because I would have liked to be her friend and listen to her stories about her job. I hoped she was a more subtle detective than she was a woman. And I had to answer the damn questions anyway, even though I knew, Mother knew, and I believe Arthur knew, that they were a waste of time.

Robin stayed the whole time, though his presence was not absolutely necessary once he'd told his simple story to the detectives. "I ran into Roe Teagarden in the grocery, and asked her if I could come over here to relax a little since my place is such a mess. When the candy came, she seemed quite surprised, yes. I also saw the hole in the bottom of the piece of candy when Mrs. Teagarden held it up. No, I didn't know either Roe or Mrs. Teagarden until the last two days. I met Mrs. Teagarden briefly when I went by her real estate office to rendezvous with the lady who was going to show me the apartment next door, and I didn't meet Roe until the Real Murders meeting last night."

"And you've been here since when?" Arthur asked quietly. He was standing in the kitchen talking to Robin, while Detective Liggett questioned Mother and me as we sat on the couch and she crouched on the love seat.

"Oh, I've been here about an hour and a half," Robin said with a slight edge.

Arthur's voice had had absolutely no overtone whatsoever (Liggett was not quite that good) but I had the distinct feeling that everyone here was following his or her own agenda, except possibly my mother. She was certainly no dummy when a sexual element entered the air, however, and in fact she suddenly gave me one of her dazzling smiles of approval, which I could have done without since Detective Liggett seemed to intercept it and interpret it as some kind of reflection on her.

My mother rose and swept up her purse and terminated the interview. "My daughter is fine and I am fine, and I cannot imagine that my former husband sent this candy or ever intended to hurt either of us," she said decisively. "He adores Aurora, and he and I have a civil relationship. Our little family habits are no secret to anyone. I don't imagine our little Christmas custom of a box of candy has gone unremarked. Probably, I've bored people many times by talking about it. We'll be interested to hear, of course, when you all find out what is actually in the candy—if anything. Maybe the holes in the bottom are just to alarm us, and this is some practical joke. Thanks for coming, and I have to be getting back to the office." I stood up too, and Lynn Liggett felt forced to walk to the door with us.

My mother got into her car first, while Arthur and Lynn conferred together on the patio. Robin was clearly undecided about what he should do. Arthur throwing out his male challenge, in however subdued a way, had struck Robin by surprise, and he was squinting thoughtfully at my stove without seeing it. He was probably wondering what he'd gotten into, and if this murder investigation was going to be as much fun as he'd anticipated.

I was abruptly sick of all of them. Maybe I hadn't been a big dating success because I was a boring person, but possibly it had been because I had limited tolerance for all this preliminary maneuvering and signal reading. My friend Amina Day loved all this stuff and was practically a professional at it. I missed Amina suddenly and desperately.

"Come have lunch with me in the city Monday," Robin suggested, having reached some internal decision.

I thought a moment. "Okay," I agreed. "I covered for another librarian when she took her kid to the orthodontist last week, so I don't have to go in Monday until two o'clock."

"Are you familiar with the university campus? Oh, sure, you went there. Well, meet me at Tarkington Hall, the English building. I'll be finishing up a writer's workshop at 11:45 on the third floor in Room 36. We'll just leave from there, if that suits you."

"That'll be fine. See you then."

"If you need me for anything, I'll be at home all day tomorrow getting ready for my classes."

"Thanks."

The phone rang inside and I turned to get it as Robin sauntered out my gate, waving a casual hand to the two detectives. An excited male voice asked for Arthur, and I called him to the phone. Lynn Liggett had recovered her cool, and when I called, "Arthur!

Phone!'' her mouth only twitched a little. Oops, silly me. Should have said Detective Smith.

I watered my rose trees while Arthur talked inside. Lynn regarded me thoughtfully. The silence between us was pretty fragile, and I felt small talk was not a good idea, but I tried anyway.

"How long have you been on the force here?" I asked.

"About three years. I came here as a patrol officer, then got promoted."

Maybe Detective Liggett and I would have become bosom buddies in a few more minutes, but Arthur came out of the apartment then with electricity crackling in every step.

"The purse has been found," he said to his co-worker.

"No shit! Where?"

"Stuffed under the front seat of a car."

Well, say which one! I almost said indignantly.

But Arthur didn't, of course, and he and his confrere were out the gate with nary a word for me. And I'll give this to Lynn Liggett, she was too involved in her work to look back at me in triumph.

To keep my hands busy while my mind roamed around, I began refinishing an old wooden two-drawer chest that I'd had in my guest bedroom for months waiting for just such a moment. After I wrestled it down the stairs and out onto the patio, the sanding turned out to be just the thing I needed.

Naturally I thought about the candy incident, and wondered if the police had called my father yet. I couldn't imagine what he'd think of all this. As I scrubbed my hands under the kitchen sink after finishing, I had a new thought, one I should have had before. Did sending the candy to Mother imitate another crime? I went to my shelves and began searching through all my "true murder" books. I couldn't find anything, so this incident wasn't patterned after one of the better-known murders. Jane Engle, my fellow librarian, had a larger personal collection than I, so I called her and told her what had happened.

"That rings a faint bell...it's an American murder, I think," Jane said interestedly. "Isn't this bizarre, Roe? That such things could happen in Lawrenceton? To us? Because I really begin to think this is happening to us, to the members of our little club. Did you hear that Mamie's purse has been found under the seat in Melanie Clark's car?"

"Melanie! Oh, I can't believe it!"

"The police may be taking that seriously, but Roe, you and I know that's ridiculous. I mean, Melanie Clark. It's a plant."

"Huh?"

"A club member was killed, and another club member is being used to divert suspicion."

"You think whoever killed Mamie took her purse and deliberately planted it under Melanie's car seat," I said slowly.

"Oh, yes." I could picture Jane standing in her tiny house full of her mother's furniture, Jane's silver chignon gleaming amid bookcases full of gory death.

"But Melanie and Gerald Wright could have had something going," I protested weakly. "Melanie could really have done it."

"Aurora, you know she's absolutely head over heels about Bankston Waites. The little house she rents is just down the street from mine and I can't help but notice his car is there a great deal." Jane tactfully didn't specify whether that included overnight.

"Her car is here a lot too," I admitted.

"So," Jane said persuasively, "I am sure that this candy thing is another old murder case revisited, and maybe the police will find the poison in another club member's kitchen!"

"Maybe," I said slowly. "Then none of us are safe."

"No," Jane said. "Not really."

"Who could have it in for us that bad?"

"My dear, I haven't the slightest. But you can bet I'll be thinking about it, and I'm going to start looking for a case like yours right this moment."

"Thanks, Jane," I said, and I hung up with much to think about, myself.

I had nothing special to do that night, as my Saturday nights had tended to run the past couple of years. Right after I ate my Saturday splurge of pizza and salad, I remembered my resolution to call Amina in Houston.

Miraculously, she was in. Amina hadn't been in on a Saturday night in twelve years, and she was going out later, she said immediately, but her date was a department store manager who worked late on Saturday.

"How is Houston?" I asked wistfully.

"Oh, it's great! So much to do! And everyone at work is so friendly." Amina was a first-rate legal secretary.

People almost always were friendly to Amina. She was a slender brown-eyed freckle-faced extrovert almost exactly my age, and I'd grown up with her and remained best friends with her through college. Amina had married and divorced childlessly, the only interruption in her long, exhaustive dating career. She was not really pretty, but she was irresistible—a laughing, chattering live wire, never at a loss for a word. She had a great talent for enjoying life and for maximizing every asset she'd been born with or acquired (her hair was not exactly naturally blond). My mother should have had Amina for a daughter, I thought suddenly.

After Amina finished telling me about her job, I dropped my bombshell.

"You found a body! Oh, yick! Who was it?" Amina shrieked. "Are you okay? Are you having bad dreams? Was the chocolate really poisoned?"

Amina being my best friend, I told her the truth. "I don't know yet if the chocolate was poisoned. Yes, I'm having bad dreams, but this is really exciting at the same time."

"Are you safe, do you think?" she asked anxiously. "Do you want to come stay with me until this is all over? I can't believe this is happening to you! You're so nice!"

"Well, nice or not," I retorted grimly, "it's happening. Thanks for asking me, Amina, and I will come to see you soon. But I have to stay here for now. I don't think I'm in any more danger. This was my turn to be targeted, I guess, and I came out okay." I skipped my speculation with Arthur that maybe the killer would go on killing, and Jane Engle's conjecture that maybe we would all be drawn in, and cut right to Amina's area of expertise.

"I have a situation here," I began, and at once had her undivided attention. The nuances and dosey-does between the sexes were Amina's bread and butter. I hadn't had anything like this to tell Amina since we were in high school. It was hard to credit that grown people still engaged in all this—foreplay.

"So," Amina said when I'd finished. "Arthur is a little resentful that this Robin spent the afternoon at

your place, and Robin's trying to decide whether he
likes you well enough to keep up the beginning of your
relationship in view of Arthur's slight proprietary air.
Though Arthur is not the proprietor of anything yet,
right?''

"Right."

"And you haven't actually had a date with either of
these bozos, right?''

"Right."

"But Robin has asked you to lunch in the city for
Monday."

"Uh-huh."

"And you're supposed to meet him at the classroom."

"Yep."

"And Lizanne has definitely discarded this Robin."
Amina and Lizanne had always had a curious relationship. Amina operated on personality and Lizanne
on looks, but they'd both run through the male population of Lawrenceton and surrounding towns at an
amazing rate.

"Lizanne formally bequeathed him to me," I told
Amina.

"She's not greedy," Amina conceded. "If she
doesn't want 'em, she lets 'em know, and she lets 'em
go. Now, if you're going to meet him at the university, you realize he's going to be sitting in a classroom

full of little chickies just panting to hop in bed with a famous writer. He's not ugly, right?''

''He's not conventionally handsome,'' I said. ''He has charm.''

''Well, don't wear one of those blouse and skirt combinations you're always wearing to work!''

''What do you suggest I wear?'' I inquired coldly.

''Listen, you called me for advice,'' Amina reminded me. ''Okay, I'm giving it to you. You've had an awful time. Nothing makes you feel better than a few new clothes, and you can afford it. So go to my mom's shop tomorrow when it opens, and get something new. Maybe a classic town 'n country type dress. Stick to little earrings, since you're so short, and maybe a few gold chains.'' (A few? I was lucky to have one my mother had given me for Christmas. Amina's boyfriends gave her gold chains for every occasion, in whatever length or thickness they could afford. She probably had twenty.) ''That should be fine for a casual lunch in the city,'' Amina concluded.

''You think he'll notice me as a woman, not just a fellow murder buff?''

''If you want him to notice you as a woman, just lust after him.''

''Huh?''

''I don't mean lick your lips or pant. Keep conversation normal. Don't do anything obvious. You have to keep it so you don't lose anything if he decides he's not interested." Amina was as interested in saving face as any Japanese.

"So what do I do?"

"Just *lust*. Keep everything going like normal, but sort of concentrate on the area below your waist and above your knees, right? And send out *waves*. You can do it. It's like the Kegel exercise. You can't show anyone how to do it, but if you describe it to a woman, she can pick it up."

"I'll try," I said doubtfully.

"Don't worry, it'll come naturally," Amina told me. "I have to hang up, the doorbell is ringing. Call me again and tell me how it goes, okay? The only thing wrong with Houston is that you aren't here."

"I miss you," I said.

"Yeah, and I miss you, but you needed me to leave," Amina said, and then she did hang up.

And after a moment's disbelief, I knew she was right. Her departure had freed me from the role of the most popular woman's best friend, a role that required I not attempt to make the most of myself because even the best of me could not compete with Amina. I almost had to be the intellectual drab one.

I was sitting thinking about what Amina had said when the phone rang while my hand was still resting on it. I jumped a mile.

"It's me again," Amina said rapidly. "Listen, Franklin is waiting for me in the living room, but I ran back here to my other phone to tell you this. You said Perry Allison was in that club with you? You watch out for Perry. When he was in college with me, he and I took a lot of the same courses our freshman year. But he would have these mood swings. He'd be hyper-excited and follow me around just jabbering, then he'd be all quiet and sullen and just stare at me. Finally the college called his mother."

"Poor Sally," I said involuntarily.

"She came and got him and I think committed him, not just because of me but because he was skipping classes and no one would room with him because his habits got so strange."

"I think he's beginning to repeat that pattern, Amina. He's still holding together at the library, but I see Sally looking worried these days."

"You just watch out for him. He never hurt anyone that I know of, though he made a bunch of people nervous. But if he's involved in this murder thing, you watch out!"

"Thanks, Amina."

"Sure, 'bye now."

And she was gone again to enjoy herself with Franklin.

SEVEN

SUNDAY DAWNED WARM and rainy. A breeze swooped over the fence and rustled my rose trees. It was not a morning to eat breakfast on the patio. I fried bacon and ate my bakery sweet roll while listening to a local radio broadcast. The mayoral candidates were answering questions on this morning's talk show. The election promised more interest than the usual Democratic shoo-in, since not only was there a Republican candidate who actually had a slim chance, there was a candidate from the—gasp—Communist Party! Of course, this was the candidate whose campaign Benjamin Greer was managing. Poor miserable Benjamin, hoping that the Communist Party and politics would be his salvation. Of course the Communist, Morrison Pettigrue, was one of the New People, one of those who'd fled the city but wanted to stay close to it.

At least this would be a unifying election for Lawrenceton. None of the candidates was black, which always made for a tense campaign and a divisive one. The Republican and Democrat were having the time of their political lives, giving sane, sober answers to banal questions, and thoroughly enjoying Pettigrue's fiery responses that sometimes bordered on the irrational.

Bless his heart, I thought sadly, not only is he a Communist but he's also very unappealing. I'd made a point of looking for Pettigrue's campaign posters on the way back from the grocery store the day before. They said nothing about the Communist Party (just "Elect Morrison Pettigrue, the People's Choice, for Mayor") and they showed him to be a grim-featured swarthy man who had obviously suffered badly from acne.

I listened while I ate breakfast, but then I switched to some country and western music for my dishwashing. Domestic chores always went faster when you could sing about drinkin' and cheatin'.

It was such a nice little morning I decided to go to church. I often did. I sometimes enjoyed it and felt better for going, but I felt no spiritual compulsion. I went because I hoped I'd "catch it," like deliberately exposing myself to the chicken pox. Sometimes I even wore a hat and gloves, though that was bordering on parody and gloves were not so easy to find anymore. It wasn't a hat-and-gloves day, today, too dark and rainy, and I wasn't in a role-playing mood, anyway.

As I pulled into the Presbyterian parking lot, I wondered if I'd see Melanie Clark, who sometimes attended. Had she been arrested? I couldn't believe stolid Melanie truly was in danger of being charged

with Mamie Wright's murder. The only possible mo-
tive anyone could attribute to Melanie was an affair
with Gerald Wright. Someone . . . some murderer, I
reminded myself . . . was playing an awful joke on
Melanie.

I drifted through the service, thinking about God
and Mamie. I felt horrible when I thought of what
another human being had done to Mamie; yet I had to
face it, when she had been alive the predominant feeling I'd had for her had been contempt. Now Mamie's
soul, and I believe we do all have one, was facing God,
as I would one day too. This was too close to the bone
for me, and I buried that thought so I could dig it up
later when I wasn't so vulnerable.

I MADE MY WAY out of church, speaking with most of
the congregation along my way. All the talk I heard
was about Melanie and her predicament, and the lat-
est information appeared to be that Melanie had had
to go down to the police station for a while, but on
Bankston's vehement vouching for her every move on
the evening of Mamie Wright's death, she'd been al-
lowed to go home and (the feeling went) was thus ex-
onerated.

Melanie herself was an orphan, but Bankston's
mother was a Presbyterian. Today of course she was
the center of an attentive group on the church steps.
Mrs. Waites was as blond and blue-eyed as her son,

and ordinarily just as phlegmatic. But this Sunday she was an angry woman and didn't care who knew it. She was mad at the police for suspecting "that sweet Melanie" for one single minute. As if a girl like that was going to beat a fly to death, much less a grown woman! And those police suggesting that maybe things weren't as they should be between Melanie and Mr. Wright! As if wild horses could drag Melanie and Bankston away from each other! At least this awful thing had gone and gotten Bankston to speak his mind. He and Melanie were going to be married in two months. No, a date hadn't been set, but they were going to decide about one today, and Melanie was going to go down to Millie's Gifts this week and pick out china and silver patterns.

This was a triumphant moment for Mrs. Waites, who had been trying to marry off Bankston for years. Her other children were settled, and Bankston's apparent willingness to wait for the right woman to come to him, instead of actively searching himself, had tried Mrs. Waites to the limit.

I would have to go pick out a fork or salad plate. I'd given lots of similar gifts in a hundred different patterns. I sighed, and tried hard not to feel sorry for myself as I drove to Mother's. I always ate Sunday lunch with her, unless she was off on one of the myriad real estate conventions she attended or out showing houses.

Mother (who had spent a rare Sunday morning at home) was in fine spirits because she'd sold a $200,000 house the day before, after she'd left my apartment. Not too many women can get poisoned chocolates, be interrogated by the police, and sell expensive properties in the same day.

"I'm trying to get John to let me list his house," she told me over the pot roast.

"What? Why would he sell his house? It's beautiful."

"His wife has been dead several years now, and all the children are gone, and he doesn't need a big house to rattle around in," my mother said.

"You've been divorced for twelve years, your child is gone, and you don't need a big house to rattle around in either," I pointed out. I had been wondering why my mother didn't unload the "four br two-story brick w/frpl and 3 baths" I'd grown up in.

"Well, there's a possibility John will have somewhere else to live soon," Mother said too casually. "We may get married."

God, everyone was doing it!

I pulled myself together and looked happy for Mother's sake. I managed to say the right things, and I meant them, and she seemed pleased.

What on earth could I get them for a wedding present?

"Since John doesn't seem to want to talk about his involvement with Real Murders right now," Mother said suddenly, "why don't you just tell me about this club?"

"John's an expert on Lizzie Borden," I explained. "If you really want to know about his main interest, apart from golf and you, it's Lizzie. You ought to read Victoria Lincoln's *A Private Disgrace*. That's one of the best books about the Borden case I've read."

"Um, Aurora . . . who was Lizzie Borden?"

I gaped at my mother. "That's like asking a baseball fan who Mickey Mantle was," I said finally. "I didn't know that a person could not know who Lizzie Borden was. Just ask John. He'll talk your ear off. But if you read the book first, he'll appreciate it."

Mother actually wrote the title in her little notebook. She really meant it about John Queensland, she was really serious about getting married. I couldn't decide how I felt; I only knew how I ought to feel. At least acting that out made my mother happy.

"Really, Aurora, I want you to tell me about the club in general, though I do want to discuss John's particular interest intelligently, of course. Now that you and he are both tied in with this horrible murder, and you and I got sent that candy, I want to know what the background on these crimes is."

"Mother, I can't remember when Real Murders started . . . about three years ago, I guess. There was a book signing at Thy Sting, the mystery book store in the city. And all of us now in Real Murders turned up for the signing, which was being held for a book about a real murder. It was such a funny coincidence, all us Lawrenceton people showing up, interested in the same thing, that we sort of agreed to call each other and start something up we could all come to in our own town. So we began meeting every month, and the format for the meetings just evolved—a lecture and discussion on a real murder most months, a related topic other months.'' I shrugged. I was getting tired of explaining Real Murders. I expected Mother to change the subject now, as she always had before when I'd tried to talk about my interest in the club.

''You told me earlier that you believe Mamie Wright's murder was patterned on the Wallace murder,'' Mother said instead. ''And you said that Jane Engle believes that the candy being sent to us is also patterned like another crime—she's trying to look it up?''

I nodded.

''You're in danger,'' my mother said flatly. ''I want you to leave Lawrenceton until this is all over. There's no way you can be implicated, like poor Melanie was with that purse hidden in her car, if you're out of town.''

''Well, that would be great, Mom,'' I said, knowing she hated to be called 'Mom', ''but I happen to have a job. I'm supposed to just go to my boss and tell him my mother is scared something might happen to me, so I have to get out of town for an indefinite period of time? Just hold my job, Mr. Clerrick?''

"Aren't you scared?'' she asked furiously.

"Yes, yes! If you had seen what this killer can do, if you had seen Mamie Wright's head, or what was left of it, you'd be scared too! But I can't leave! I have a life!''

My mother didn't say anything, but her unguarded response, which showed clearly in those amazing eyebrows, was "Since when?"

I went home with a plateful of leftovers for supper, as usual, and decided to have a Sunday afternoon and evening of self-pity. Sunday afternoons are good for that. I took off my pretty dress (no matter what Amina says, I do have some pretty and flattering clothes) and put on my nastiest sweats. I stopped short of washing off my makeup and messing up my hair, but I felt that way.

What I hated to do most was wash windows, so I decided today was the day. The clouds had lightened a little and I no longer expected rain, so I collected all the window washing paraphernalia and did the downstairs, grimly spraying and wiping and then repeating the process. I carried around my step stool, even with its boost barely reaching the top panes. When they were shining clearly, I trudged upstairs with my

cleaning rag and spray bottle and began on the guest
bedroom. It overlooked the parking lot, so I had a
great view of the elderly couple next door, the Crandalls, coming home in their Sunday best. Perhaps
they'd been to a married child's for lunch . . . they had
several children here in town, and I recalled Teentsy
Crandall mentioning at least eight grandchildren.
Teentsy and her husband Jed were laughing together,
and he patted her on the shoulder as he held open the
gate. No sooner were they inside than Bankston's blue
car entered the lot and he and Melanie emerged holding hands and smoldering at each other. Even to me,
and I am not really experienced, it was apparent that
they could hardly wait until they got inside.

As a crowning touch to a feel-sorry-for-yourself afternoon, it could hardly be beat. What did I have to
look forward to? I asked myself rhetorically. *60 Minutes* and heated-up pot roast.

I decided I'd take Amina's advice after all. I'd be
there when her mom's shop opened at 10:00 the next
morning. With luck and my charge card, I could be
ready for my trip to the city to have lunch with Robin
Crusoe.

Then I decided that there was, after all, something
I could do with my evening. I picked up my personal
phone book and began dialling.

EIGHT

By 8:00 THEY WERE all there. It was crowded in my apartment, with Jane, Gerald, and Sally given the best seats and the others perched on chairs from the dinette set or sitting on the floor, like the lovebirds, Melanie and Bankston. I hadn't called Robin, because he had only been to Real Murders one time; one disastrous time. LeMaster Cane was sitting apart from everyone else, speaking to no one, his dark face deliberately blank. Gifford had brought Reynaldo, and they were huddled together with their backs pressed against the wall, looking sullen. Gerald still looked shocked, his pouchy face white and strained. Benjamin Greer was trying to be buddies with Perry Allison, who was openly sneering. Sally was trying not to watch her son, and carrying on a sporadic conversation with Arthur, who looked exhausted. John's creamy white head was bent toward Jane, who was talking quietly.

Even under the circumstances, I was sorely tempted to stand and say, "I guess you're wondering why I called you all here," but I didn't quite have the nerve. And after all, they knew why they were here.

I had assumed John would take the lead, since he was the president of our club. But he was looking at me expectantly, and I realized that it was up to me to start.

"Friends," I said loudly, and the little rags of conversation stopped as though they'd been trimmed off with a knife. I paused for a minute, trying to marshall my thoughts, and Gifford said, "Stand up so we can see ya."

I saw several nods, so I stood. "First," I resumed, "I want to tell Gerald we're all sorry, grieved, about Mamie." Gerald looked around listlessly, acknowledging the murmur of sympathy with a nod of his head.

"Then," I went on, "I think we need to talk about what's happening to us." I had everyone's undivided attention. "I guess you all know about the tampered-with candy sent to me and my mother. I can't say poisoned, because we don't know for sure it was; so I can't be sure the intent was to kill. But I suppose we can assume that." I looked around to see if anyone would disagree. No one did. "And of course you all also know that Mamie's purse was put in Melanie's car."

Melanie looked down in embarrassment, her straight dark hair swinging forward to hide her face. Bankston put his arm around her and held her close. "As if Melanie would do such a thing," he said hotly.

"Well, we all know that," I said.

"Of course," Jane chimed indignantly.

"I know," I went on very very carefully, "that Sally and Arthur are in a delicate position tonight. Sally might want to report to the paper that we met, and Arthur will have to tell the police that he was here and what happened. I can see that. But I hope that Sally will agree that tonight is off the record."

Everyone looked at Sally, who threw back her bronze head and glared at us all. "The police want me not to print that the murder was a copy," she said in exasperation. "But everyone in Real Murders has been telling other people anyway. I'm losing the best story I ever had. Now you all want me to not be a reporter tonight. It's like asking Arthur not to be a policeman for a couple of hours."

"Then you won't keep this off the record?" Gifford said unexpectedly. "'Cause if this isn't off the record, I'm out the door." He stared at Sally, and smoothed back his long hair.

"Oh, all right," Sally said. Her tan eyes snapped as she glared around the room. "But I'm telling you all, this is the last time anything said to me about these murders is off the record!"

That reduced us all to speechlessness for a moment.

"Just what did you want us here for, dear?" Jane asked.

Good question. I took the plunge.

"It's probably one of us, right?" I said nervously.

No one moved. No one turned to look at the person beside him.

A presence in the room gathered power in that silence. That presence was fear, of course. We were all afraid, or getting there.

"But it may be an enemy of someone here," said Arthur finally.

"So, who has enemies?" I inquired. "I know that sounds naive, but for God's sake, we have to think, or we'll be mired in this until someone else dies."

"I think you're overstating this," said Melanie. She actually had a little social smile on her lips.

"How, Melanie?" asked Perry suddenly. "How could Roe possibly be overstating this? We all know what's happened. We sure don't have to be geniuses to figure out that Mamie's murder was meant to be like Julia Wallace's. One of us is nuts. And we all know from reading so much about it, that a psychotic murderer can be as nice as pie on the outside and a screaming loony inside. What about Ted Bundy?"

"I just meant—" Melanie began uncertainly, "I just meant that maybe, I don't know, someone we don't know is doing this, and it really isn't tied in to us at all. Maybe the presence of a group like ours sparked all this in someone's mind."

"Maybe pigs can fly," muttered Reynaldo, and Gifford laughed.

It wasn't a normal laugh, and the presence was bumping and flopping around the room like a blind thing, ready to grab the first person it lit on. Everyone was getting more and more nervous. I had made a mistake, and we were accomplishing nothing.

"If any one of you does have an enemy, someone who knows about your membership in Real Murders, someone who, maybe, has been reading your club handouts or reading your books, getting interested in what we study, now is the time for you to think of that person," I said. "If we can't come up with someone like that, then this is the last meeting of Real Murders."

This brought another silence, that of shocked realization.

"Of course," breathed Jane Engle. "This is the end of us."

"It may be the end, literally, of more of us if we can't figure this out," Sally said bluntly. "Whoever this is, is going to go on. Can any of you see this stopping? It isn't in the picture. Someone's having a great time, and I'd put my money on it being someone in this room."

"I for one have better things to do than sit in a room with all these accusations going around," Benjamin said. "I'm in politics now, and I would have quit Real

Murders anyway. Don't anyone come trying to kill me, that's all, because I'll be waiting for him."

He left amid uneasy whispering, and before he was quite out my back door, Gifford said audibly, "Benjamin isn't worth killing. What an asshole."

We were all feeling some permutation on that theme, I imagine.

"I'm sorry," I said to everyone. "I thought I could accomplish something. I thought if we were all together, we could remember something that would help solve this horrible murder."

Everyone began to shift slightly, preparing to gather up whatever or whoever they'd come with.

John Queensland exhibited an unexpected sense of drama.

"The last meeting of Real Murders is now adjourned," he said formally.

NINE

I LOOKED WONDERFUL. Amina's mom had nodded thoughtfully when I told her I needed something new to wear to lunch in the city, and it had to be something I could wear to work too. Amina hadn't told me to add that, but Amina wasn't paying the bill. Mrs. Day flicked the laden hangers with a professional hand. She glanced from blouses to me with narrowed eyes, while I tried not to look as silly (or as hopeful) as I felt.

She extracted an ivory blouse with dark green vines twining up it, and a dark green bow ("At your age, honey, you don't need a bright one, too young") that nestled in the wild waves of my hair with definite femininity. I got khaki-colored pants with a wide belt and extravagant pleats, and shoes too. I slipped them on to wear away from the store. Mrs. Day clucked over my lipstick (not dark enough), but I stuck by my guns. I hated dark lipstick.

This was not a showy outfit, but it was a definite change for me. I felt great, and as I drove the mile out of town that got me to the interstate circling the city, I felt quite confident Robin would be impressed.

I felt less certain when I peeked through the one glass pane in the classroom door. As Amina had predicted, there were lots of cute college "chickies" in Robin's creative writing workshop. I was willing to bet seven out of nine wrote poetry that dealt with world hunger and bitter endings to relationships. At least five weren't wearing bras. The four men in the workshop were of the serious and scraggly variety. They probably wrote existential plays. Or poetry about bitter endings to relationships.

When the rest rose to leave, two of the cute chickies lingered to fascinate Robin. I was smiling, thinking of Amina as I went into the classroom.

Robin naturally thought the grin was for him. He beamed back. "Glad you found the room okay," he said, and the young women—I reminded myself they were not girls—turned to stare at me. "Lisa, Kimberly, this is Aurora Tea-garden." Oh, I hadn't seen that one coming. Robin and his good manners. The brunette looked incredulous, and the streaky blond sniggered before she could stop herself.

"Are you ready for lunch?" Robin asked, and their faces straightened in a jiffy.

Thanks, Robin. "Yes, let's go," I said clearly, smiling all the while.

"Sure. Well, I'll see you in class Wednesday," he told Lisa and Kimberly. They sauntered out with their armfuls of books, and Robin tossed a couple of anthologies into his briefcase. "Let me just stow this in my office," he said. His office was right across the hall, and was full of books and papers, but not his, Robin explained. "James Artis was supposed to teach three writers' workshops and one class on the history of the mystery novel. But when he had a heart attack, he recommended me."

"Why'd you take it?" I asked. We strolled across campus companionably, heading for a salad and sandwich restaurant just down the street.

"I needed a change," he said. "I was tired of being shut up in a room writing all day. I'd written three books in a row with little or no break in between, I had no exciting ideas for my next book, and teaching just sounded interesting. James recommended Lawrenceton as a place where I wouldn't have to go broke paying rent, and after I'd been staying in a vacant visitor's room in one of the men's dorms for a couple of weeks, I was grateful to find the townhouse."

"Are you planning on staying for any length of time?" I asked delicately.

"That depends on the success of the workshops and the class," he said, "and James's health. Even if I leave the university, I might stay in the area. So far I like it here just as well as the place I was living before. I don't really have ties anywhere anymore. My parents have retired to Florida, so I don't have a reason to go back to my home town . . . St. Louis,'' he said in answer to my unspoken question.

He held open the door to the restaurant. It was a ferny place, with waiters and waitresses in matching aprons and blue jeans. Our waiter's name was Don, and he was happy to serve us today. A local ''mellow'' rock listening station was being piped in for all us old rockers, who ranged in age from twenty-eight to forty-two. As we were looking at the menus, I decided to start lusting, as per Amina's instructions. While we ordered, I seemed to get it misdirected, for Don got pretty red in the face and kept trying to look down my blouse. Robin seemed to be receiving the brunt of it though. He rather hesitantly (high noon, public place, had to teach a class that afternoon) took my hand across the table.

I never knew how to react to that. My thoughts always ran, Wow, he took my hand, does that mean he wants to go to bed with me, or date me more, or what? And I never knew where to look. Into his eyes? Too challenging. At his hand? Pretty stupid. And was I supposed to move my hand to clasp his? Uncomfortable. I never *was* much good at this.

Our salads arrived, so we unhitched hands and picked up our forks with some relief. I was wondering whether I should try to keep on lusting while I ate, when I realized James Taylor had trailed to an end and the news was starting. The name of my town always made me pay attention. A neutral woman's voice was saying, "In other news, Lawrenceton mayoral candidate Morrison Pettigrue was found slain today. Pettigrue, thirty-five, was campaigning as the candidate of the Communist Party. His campaign manager, Benjamin Greer, found Pettigrue dead of stab wounds in the bathtub of his Lawrenceton home. Sheets of paper were floating in the water, but police would not say whether any of those sheets contained a suicide note. Police have no suspects in the slaying, and declined to speculate on whether the killing was, as Greer claims, a political assassination."

Our forks poised in midair, Robin and I stared at each other like stricken loonies, and not in lust either.

"In the tub," Robin said.

"With a knife. And the paper clinches it."

"Marat," we said in unison.

"Poor Benjamin," I said on my own. He'd rejected us, launched on his own new direction, and gotten kicked in the nuts.

"Smith would recognize it, right?" Robin asked me after some fruitless speculation on our part.

"I think so," I said confidently. "Arthur's smart and well-read."

"Did you ever find out if the chocolates fit a pattern?"

"It rang a bell with Jane Engle," I told him, and then had to explain who she was and why her memory was reliable. He'd only met the members of Real Murders once. "She's looking for the right case."

"Do you think she'll know by tomorrow night?" he asked.

"Well, I may see her today. Maybe she will have found something by then."

"Is there a nice restaurant in Lawrenceton?"

"Well, there's the Carriage House." It was a real carriage house, and required a reservation; the only place in Lawrenceton that had the pretensions to do so. I offered the names of a few more places, but the Carriage House had struck his fancy.

"This lunch is a washout, we haven't eaten half our salad," he pointed out. "Let me take you out tomorrow night, and we'll have time to talk and eat."

"Why, thanks. Okay. The Carriage House is a dressy place," I added, and wondered if the hint offended him.

"Thanks for warning me," Robin said to my relief. "I'll walk you back to your car."

When I glanced at my watch, I saw he was right. All this walking, lusting, and speculation had used up as much time as I had, and I'd just make it to work on time.

"If you don't mind making our reservation, I'll pick you up tomorrow at 7:00," Robin said as we reached my car.

Well, we had another date, though I didn't think it was strictly a social date. Robin had a professional interest in these murders, I figured, and I was the local who could interpret the scene for him. But he gave me a peck on the cheek as I eased into my car, and I drove back to Lawrenceton singing James Taylor.

That was much nicer than picturing dark, scowling, acne-scarred Morrison Pettigrue turning the bath water scarlet with his blood.

TEN

"CORDELIA BOTKIN, 1898," Jane hissed triumphantly.

She'd come up behind me as I was reshelving books that had been checked in. I was at the end of a stack close to the wall, about to wheel my cart around the end and onto the next row. I drew in a breath down low in my chest, shut my eyes, and prayed to forgive her. Tuesday morning had been going so well.

"Roe, I'm so sorry! I thought you must have heard me coming."

I shook my head. I tried not to lean on the cart so obviously.

"Cordelia who?" I finally managed to say.

"Botkin. It's close enough. It doesn't actually fit, but it's close enough. This was so sloppy that I think it was an afterthought, or maybe this was even supposed to come off before Mamie Wright was killed."

"You're probably right, Jane. The box of candy took six days to get here, and it was mailed from the city, so whoever sent it probably thought I'd get it in two or three days."

I glanced around to see if anyone was in earshot. Lillian Schmidt, another librarian, was shelving books a few stacks away, but she wasn't actually within hearing distance.

"How does it fit, Jane?"

Jane flipped open the notebook she always seemed to have with her. "Cordelia Botkin lived in San Francisco. She became the mistress of the Associated Press bureau chief, John Dunning. He'd left a wife back in..." Jane scanned her notes, "...Dover, Delaware. Botkin mailed the wife several anonymous letters first, did your mother get any?"

I nodded. With a very stiff upper lip, Mother had told Lynn Liggett something she'd never thought significant enough to tell me: she'd gotten an incomprehensible and largely nasty anonymous letter in the mail a few days before the candy came. She'd thought the incident so ugly and meaningless that she hadn't wanted to "upset" me with it. She had thrown it away, of course, but it had been typed.

I was willing to bet it had been typed on the same machine that had typed the mailing label on the package.

"Anyway," Jane continued after checking her notes, "Cordelia finally decided Dunning was going back to his wife, so she poisoned some bonbons and mailed them to Dunning's wife. The wife and a friend of hers died."

"Died," I said slowly.

Jane nodded, tactfully keeping her eyes on her notes. "Your father is still in newspapers, isn't he, Roe?"

"Yes, he's not a reporter, but he's head of the advertising department."

"And he's living with his new wife, which could be said to represent 'another woman'."

"Well, yes."

"So obviously the murderer saw the outline was roughly the same and seized the opportunity."

"Did you tell Arthur Smith about this?"

"I thought I had better," Jane said, with a wise nod of her head.

"What did he say?" I asked.

"He wanted to know which book I'd gotten my information from, wrote that down, thanked me, looked harassed, and told me goodbye. I got the impression he's having trouble convincing his superiors about the significance of these murders. What was in the candy, do you know yet?"

"No, they took the box to the state lab for analysis. Arthur warned us that some of the tests take quite a while."

Lillian was moving closer and looking curious, a chronic state with Lillian. But all my co-workers were regarding me with more than normal interest. A quiet librarian finds a body at the meeting of a pretty odd club on Friday night, gets a box of doctored chocolates in the mail on Saturday, turns up dressed in all-new and uncharacteristic clothes on Monday, has a whispered conference with an excited woman on Tuesday.

"I'd better go. I'm disturbing you at work," Jane whispered. She knew Lillian quite well. "But I was so excited when I tracked down the pattern, I just had to run down here and tell you. Of course, the Communist man's murder was patterned after the Marat assassination. Poor Benjamin Greer! He found the body, the newscast said."

"Jane, I appreciate your researching this for me," I hissed back. "I'll take you out to lunch next week to thank you." The last thing I wanted to talk about was Morrison Pettigrue's murder.

"Oh, my goodness, that's not necessary. You gave me something to do for a while. Substituting at the school and filling in here are interesting, but nothing has been as much fun in a long time as tracking down the right murder. However, I suspect I will have to get a new hobby. All these deaths, all this fear. This is getting too close to the bone for me." And Jane sighed, though whether over the deaths of Mamie Wright and Morrison Pettigrue, or because she had to find a new hobby, I could not tell.

I was on the second floor of the library, which is a large gallery running around three walls and overlooking the ground floor, where the children's books, periodicals, and circulation desk are located. I was watching Jane stride out the front door and thinking about Cordelia Botkin when I recognized someone else who was exiting. It was Detective Lynn Liggett. The library director, Sam Clerrick, seemed to be walking her to the door. This struck me unpleasantly. I could only suppose that Lynn Liggett had been at the library asking questions about me. Maybe she had wanted to know my work hours? More about my character? How long I had been at work that day?

Filled with uneasy speculation, I rounded the corner of the next stack. I began shelving books automatically, still brooding over Detective Liggett's visit to the library. There was nothing bad Sam Clerrick could tell her about me, I reasoned. I was a conscientious employee. I was always on time, and I almost never got sick. I had never yelled at a member of the public, no matter how I'd been tempted—especially by parents who dumped their children at the library in the summer with instructions to amuse themselves for a couple of hours while mommy and daddy went shopping.

So why was I worried? I lectured myself. I was just seeing the down side of being involved in a criminal investigation. It was practically my civic duty not to mind being the object of police scrutiny.

I wondered if I could reasonably be considered a suspect in Mamie's murder. I could have done it, of course. I'd been home unobserved for at least an hour or more before I left for the meeting. Maybe one of the other tenants could vouch for my car being in its accustomed place, though that wouldn't be conclusive proof. And I supposed if I could have found a place that sold Mrs. See's, I could have mailed myself the candy. I could have typed the label on one of the library typewriters. Maybe Detective Liggett had been getting typing samples from all the machines! Though if the samples did match the label, it wouldn't be proof that I typed it myself. And if the sample didn't match, I could have used another machine—maybe one in my mother's office?

Now the murder of Morrison Pettigrue was another kettle of fish entirely. I had never met Mr. Pettigrue, and now never would. I hadn't known where he lived until one of the other librarians had told me, but I couldn't prove either of those things, now that I came to think about it. Ignorance is hard to prove. Besides, if he'd been killed late Sunday night after the abortive last meeting of Real Murders, I had no alibi at all. I'd been home alone feeling sorry for myself.

However, if by some miracle the killing could be proved to have occurred during the hour we were all together, we'd all be cleared! That would be too good to be true.

I was so busy trying to imagine all the pros and cons of arresting me that I bumped into Sally Allison, literally. She was looking at the books on needlework, of which the library had scores, Lawrenceton being a hell of a town for needlework.

I murmured an apology. Sally murmured back, "Don't think about it," but then she stayed glued to her spot, her eyes all too pointedly on the titles in front of her. The past couple of months, Sally has been a frequent patron of the library, even during what I supposed were her working hours. I didn't think she came to check out books, though she did leave with some every time. I was convinced she was checking on Perry. I wasn't surprised after what Amina had told me. Sometimes Sally didn't even speak to her son, I'd noticed, but eyed him from a distance, as if watching for some sign of trouble.

"How's your mother, Roe?" Sally asked.

"Just fine, thank you."

"Gotten over your scare about the candy? I didn't get to ask you last night."

Sally had called both Mother and me for an interview when she'd read the police blotter after the candy incident. Mother and I separately had been as brief as was congruent with courtesy, we discovered later when we compared notes. I thought my name had been in the paper enough recently, and Mother thought the whole incident too sordid to discuss. (Mother also, in her career-woman mode, thought an attempted poisoning would be bad for business.)

"Sally, I wasn't scared, because I didn't know then and I don't know now that someone was actually trying to hurt me or my mother. I'm going to say frankly, Sally, that you're my friend and you're a reporter, and I'm not sure recently just who I'm talking to."

Sally turned to face me. She was not angry, but she was determined. "Being a reporter on a small newspaper doesn't mean I'm not a real reporter, Roe. You're a Teagarden, so what happens to you is doubly news. Your mother is a very prominent woman in this town, and your father is a well-known man. The owner of our newspaper will not keep this police gag order agreement much longer. Does that answer your question? Lillian's coming. Have you read this book on bargello?"

I blinked and recovered. "Now, Sally, I can't sew on a button. You'd have to ask Mother if you want to know about needlework. Or Lillian," I added brilliantly, as my co-worker wheeled her own cart past the other end of the stack.

Lillian, whose ears are as fine-tuned as a bat's, heard her own name and turned in, and right away she and Sally were embroiled in an incomprehensible conversation about French knots and candlewicking. A little sadly, I returned to my shelving. When I was no longer news, I wondered whether Sally would decide she was just a friend again.

When I looked at my watch and discovered it was four o'clock and I was due to get off at six, I realized I'd better think about what I was going to wear to the Carriage House with Robin. He had mentioned picking me up at seven, which gave me a scant hour to get home, shower, redo my makeup, and dress. Reservations had been no problem; Tuesday was not a heavy night at the Carriage House, and I'd told them 7:15. Now I had to decide what to wear. My dark blue silk was back from the cleaner's. Had I ever taken the matching sandals to be repaired after I noticed the strap coming loose? Desperately I wished I had bought the black heels I'd seen at Amina's mom's shop that morning. They'd had bows on the back of the heel, and I'd thought they were ravishing. Would I have time to run by and get them?

Gradually I became aware that someone was humming on the other side of my stack with a droning, bee-like monotony. It could only be Lillian. Sure enough, when I pulled out a veterinarian's "humorous look at life with animals in and out of the house" which had been thrown in with the 364's, Lillian's round face was visible through the gap.

"I think we should be earning more money," Lillian said sulkily, "and I think we should be asked before being scheduled to work nights, and I think they should never have hired that new head librarian."

"Sam Clerrick? Nights?" I said foolishly, not knowing where to begin with my questions. Lillian had been a big Sam Clerrick fan before this moment, to the best of my knowledge. Mr. Clerrick seemed intelligent and tough to me, but I was reserving judgment on his ability to manage people.

"Oh, you haven't heard," Lillian said with pleasure. "What with all the excitement in your life lately, I guess you haven't had too much time to pay attention to ordinary everyday stuff."

I rolled my eyes to the ceiling, "Lillian, what?"

Lillian wriggled her heavy shoulders in anticipation. "You know, the Board of Trustees met two nights ago? Of course, Sam Clerrick was there, and he told them that in his view staying open at night hadn't been tried sufficiently four years ago, when it was such a flop—you remember? He wants to reinstate it for a time, with the present staff. So instead of being open one night a week we'll be open three, for a four-month trial."

Four years ago Lawrenceton had been a smaller town, and remaining open more than one night a week past six o'clock had only resulted in a higher electric bill and some bored librarians. Our one late night was a token bow to people who worked odd hours and couldn't get to the library any other time. Business had been picking up on that night, I thought fairly, and in view of Lawrenceton's recent population boom, another try at night opening was reasonable. Still, I felt mildly perturbed at the change in my schedule.

On the other hand, it was hard to regard my job as the most important thing in my life lately.

"How's he going to do it without increasing staff?" I asked without much interest.

"Instead of being on two librarians at a time, we'll be on in terms of librarian and volunteer on an open night.'

The volunteers were a mixed bunch. Mostly they tended to be older men and middle-aged to elderly women who really enjoyed books and felt at home in a library. Once they'd been trained, they were a godsend, except the very small percentage who'd taken the job to see their friends and gossip. That small percentage soon got bored and quit the program, anyway.

"I'm game," I told Lillian.

"We're going to find out more about it officially today," Lillian went on, looking disappointed at my mild reaction. "There's a staff meeting at 5:30, so Perry Allison's going to relieve you at the circulation desk. Hey," and Lillian looked at her watch obviously, "isn't it time for you to get down there now?"

"Yes, Lillian, I see that it is," I said with elaborate patience, "and I am going." We took turns on circulation as we did on almost every job, since the staff was too small for much specialization but definitely full of individuals who didn't hesitate to make their preferences known. I was darned if I was going to scurry downstairs because Lillian had looked at her watch, so I continued, "I'm willing to give night hours another shot. More time off during the day might be nice, too." *Since my night social calendar is not exactly crowded,* but I didn't feel it necessary to share that thought with Lillian.

I was relieved that the meeting wasn't going to be after the official library closing at 6:00. I suddenly recalled for sure that the sandals that went with the blue silk dress had a broken strap. "Crumbs," I muttered, shelving the last book on my cart with such force that one on the opposite side shot out and landed on the floor.

"My goodness," said Lillian triumphantly as she bent to retrieve it. "What's put us in such a snit, huh?"

I said something besides "crumbs," but I only moved my lips.

I USUALLY ENJOYED my tour in Circulation. I got to stand at the big desk to one side of the main entrance. I answered questions and accepted the books, taking the fines if the books were overdue, sliding their cards back in and putting them on book carts for transportation back to their shelves. Or I checked the books out. If there was a lot of traffic, I got a helper.

Today was a slow day, which was good since my mind wouldn't stay on my work but meandered down its own path. How close my mother had come to eating a piece of that candy. How Mamie's head had looked from the back. How glad I was I hadn't seen the front. Whether the importance of being the *finder of the body* had given Benjamin a new lease on life after the death of his political ambitions. How pleased I was about going out with Robin that night. How exciting I found Arthur Smith's blue eyes.

I yanked my thoughts away from this half-pleasant half-frightening stream of thought to exchange desultory conversation with the volunteer sitting with me at the checkout desk: Lizanne Buckley's father Arnie, a 66-year-old white-haired retiree with a mind like a steel trap. Once Mr. Buckley grew interested in a subject, he read everything he could find about it, and he forgot precious little of what he read. When he was through with that subject, he was through for good, but he remained a semi-authority on it. Mr. Buckley confessed on this warmish sleepy afternoon that he was beginning to find it difficult to find a new subject to research. I asked him how he's found them before, and he said it had always happened naturally.

"For example, I see a bee on my roses. I say to myself, Gee! Isn't that bee smaller than the one over on that rose? Are they the same kind of bee? Does this kind only get pollen from roses? Why aren't there more roses growing wild if bees carry rose pollen all over? So I read up on bees, and maybe roses. But lately, I don't know, nothing seems to jump out and grab me."

I sympathized and suggested now that warmer weather would permit him to take more walks, a new subject would present itself.

"In view of what's been happening in this town recently," Mr. Buckley commented, "I thought it might be interesting to research murderers."

I looked at him sharply, but he wasn't trying to hint about the involvement of Real Murders members in the series of crimes.

"Why don't you do that?" I asked after a minute.

"The books are all checked out," he said.

"What?"

"Almost all the nonfiction books about murder and murderers are out," he elaborated patiently.

That wasn't so startling, once I had time to mull it over. All the members of Real Murders—all the former members of Real Murders—were undoubtedly boning up and preparing themselves however they could for what might happen.

But someone might be boning up to make the happening occur.

That was sickening. I looked it in the face for a second, then had to turn away. I could not visualize, did not dare to visualize, someone I knew poring over books, trying to select what old murder to imitate next, what terrible act to re-create on the body of someone he knew.

Perry came to the desk to relieve me so I could attend the meeting, which seemed so irrelevant I almost picked up my sweater and walked out the front door instead. I had a date tonight, too. Suddenly my pleasure in that date was ashes in my mouth. At least part of my bleak mood could be written up to Perry; he was definitely in the throes of one of his downswings. His lips were set in a sullen line, the parentheses from nose to mouth deeper.

I felt sorry for Perry suddenly, and said, "Hi, see you later," as warmly as I could as I passed him on my way to the conference room. I regretted the warmth as he smiled in return. I wished he had stayed sullen. His smile was as vicious and meaningless as a shark's. I could imagine Perry as the Victorian poseur Neal Cream, giving prostitutes poison pills and then hanging around, hoping to watch them swallow.

"Go along to the meeting now," he said nastily.

I gladly left as Arnie Buckley began the uphill battle of making conversation with Perry.

With no enthusiasm at all, I slumped in a dreadful metal chair in the library conference room and heard the news that was already stale. Mr. Clerrick, with his usual efficiency and lack of knowledge of the human race, had already prepared the new duty charts and he distributed them on the spot, instead of giving everyone the chance to digest and discuss the new schedule.

I was down for Thursday night from six to nine, with Mr. Buckley penciled in tentatively as my volunteer; the volunteers hadn't yet been asked individually if they were willing to work nights, though the volunteer president had agreed in principle. Mr. Clerrick was going to put an advertisement in the newspaper telling our patrons the exciting news. (He actually said that.)

"Going out with our new resident writer tonight?" Perry inquired smoothly when I returned to the check-in desk.

He took me by surprise; my mind had been firmly on work; for once.

"Yes," I said bluntly, without thought. "Why?"

I'd let my distaste show; a mistake. I should have kept the surface of things amiable.

"Oh, no reason," Perry said airily, but he began to smile, a smile so false and disagreeable that for the first time I felt a little afraid.

"I'll take the desk now," I said. "You can go back to your work." I didn't smile and my voice was flat; it was too late now to patch it up. For an awful minute I didn't think he'd go, that the terrible gloom in Perry's head made him utterly reckless of keeping the surface of his life sewn together.

"See you later," Perry said, with no smile at all.

I watched him go with goosebumps on my arms.

"Did he say something nasty to you, Roe?" asked Mr. Buckley. He looked as pugnacious as a tiny old man with white hair can look.

"Not really. It's the way he said it," I answered, wanting to be truthful but not wanting to upset Lizanne's father.

"That boy's got snakes in his head," Mr. Buckley pronounced.

"I think you must be right. Now about this new schedule . . ."

We were soon busy again, and the surface of things was restored; but I thought Perry Allison did indeed have snakes in his head, and that his mother's frequent calls at the library were monitoring visits. Sally Allison was aware of the snakes, frightened they might slither through the widening holes in Perry's mental state.

Mr. Buckley and I were kept busy until closing time, with a spate of "patrons" of all ages, coming in to do schoolwork, returning books after they'd left work. Being busy made me feel more like myself again, more like there was a point to what I was doing.

Arthur Smith was waiting by my car. I was so intent on getting home to get ready, and was so short on time, that I was more miffed than glad to see him at first.

"I hated to interrupt you at work unless I had to," he said in his serious way.

"It's all right, Arthur. Do you have any news for me?" I thought perhaps the lab had analyzed whatever was in the chocolates.

"No, the lab work hasn't come back yet. Do you have any time?"

"Um . . . well, a few minutes."

To my pleasure, he didn't look surprised at my lack of time.

"Well, come sit in my car, or walk with me down the block."

I elected to walk, not wanting Lillian Schmidt to see mc in a car with a man in the parking lot, for some reason. So we strolled down the sidewalk in the cooling of the evening. I can't keep up with some men since my legs are so short that they have to slow considerably but Arthur seemed to adapt well.

"What did you expect of that meeting Sunday night?" he asked abruptly.

"I don't know what I expected. A miracle. I wanted someone to have an idea that would make the whole nightmare go away. Instead, someone went out and killed Morrison Pettigrue. My meeting really worked, huh?"

"That death was planned before the meeting. What bites me is that I sat there in the same room with whoever killed that man, hours before he did it, and I didn't feel a thing. Even knowing a murderer was in that room . . ." He stopped, shook his head violently, and kept walking.

"Do the other police believe what you do, that one person is doing all this?"

"I'm having a hard time convincing some of the other detectives about the similarities of these two cases to old murders. And since the Pettigrue murder, they're even less inclined to listen, even though when I saw the scene I told them myself it was like the assassination of Jean-Paul Marat. They almost laughed. There are so many right-wing loonies who might want to kill an avowed Communist, only one or two of the other detectives are willing to accept that all these incidents are related."

"I saw Lynn Liggett at the library today. I guess she was checking up on me."

"We're checking up on anyone remotely involved," Arthur said flatly. "Liggett's just doing her job. I'm supposed to find out where you were Sunday night."

"After the meeting?"

He nodded.

"At home. In bed. Alone. You know I didn't have anything to do with Mamie's death, or the chocolates, or Morrison Pettigrue's murder."

"I know. I saw you when you found Mrs. Wright's body."

I felt a ridiculous flood of warmth and gratitude at being believed.

It was already late, and I did have to get ready, so I ventured, "Is there anything else you wanted to see me about?"

"I'm a divorced man without any children," Arthur said abruptly.

Taken aback, I nodded. I tried to look intelligently inquiring.

"One of the reasons I got divorced ... my wife couldn't stand the fact that in police work, sometimes things came up and I couldn't make it on time for something we'd planned. Even in Lawrenceton, which is not New York or even Atlanta, right?"

He paused for a response, so I said, "Right," uncertainly.

"So, I want to go out with you." Those hard blue eyes turned on me with devastating effect. "But things will come up, and sometimes you'll be disappointed. You'd have to understand beforehand, if you want to go out with me too. I don't know if you do, but I wanted to get this all out front."

I thought: (a) this was admirably frank, (b) did this guy have an ego, or what?, (c) since he had said, "I don't know if you do," there was hope for him, though it had probably been just a sop thrown in my direction, and (d) I did want to go out with him, but not from a position of weakness. Arthur was a strength-respecter.

It took me a few moments to work this through. A few days before, I would have said, "Okay," meekly, but since then I had weathered a few storms and it seemed to me I could manage better for myself.

I watched my feet pacing along the sidewalk as I said, "If you're saying you want to go out with me, but that anything you're doing is more important than plans we might make, I can't agree to abide by such a lopsided—understanding." I watched my feet move steadily. Arthur's shoes were shiny and black and would last maybe twenty years. "Now, if you're saying the police department has priority in a crisis, I can see that. If you're not just providing a blanket excuse in advance to cover any time you just might feel like not showing up." I took a deep breath. So far those shoes had not marched off in another direction. "Okay. Also, this is sounding very—exclusive, since we haven't even been out yet. I would like to handle this one date at a time."

I'd underestimated Arthur.

"I must have sounded too egotistical to swallow," he said. "I'm sorry. Will you go out with me one time?"

"Okay," I said. Then I didn't know what to do. I looked sideways at him and he was smiling. "What did I say 'okay' to?" I asked.

"Unless I get assigned something I have to do, you have to remember this department is in the middle of a murder investigation..." As if I was going to forget! "...Saturday night? I've got a popcorn popper and a VCR."

No first dates at a man's apartment. By God, he could take me out someplace the first time. I didn't feel like wrestling right away. My experience was limited, but I knew that much. Besides, with Arthur I might not wrestle, and I didn't want to start a relationship that way.

"I want to go roller skating," I said out of the blue.

Arthur couldn't have looked more stunned if I'd told him I wanted to jump off the library roof. Why had I said that? I hadn't gone skating in years. I'd be black and blue and make a klutz of myself in the bargain.

But maybe he would too.

"That's original," Arthur said slowly. "You really want to do that?"

Stuck with it, I nodded grimly.

"Okay," he said firmly. "I'll pick you up at six, Saturday night. If that's all right. Then after we harm ourselves enough, we can go out to eat. All this is assuming I can have an evening off in the middle of three investigations. But maybe we'll have it wrapped up by then."

"Fine," I said. I could accept that.

We'd circled the block, so we parted at our respective cars. I watched Arthur pull out of the parking lot, and saw he was shaking his head to himself. I laughed out loud.

I HATED BEING LATE and I was late for my date with Robin. I had to ask him to wait downstairs while I put on the finishing touches.

I'd bought the shoes and I was enchanted with myself. Robin didn't seem surprised or put out at having to wait; but I felt rude and at a disadvantage, as if I should have something better to show as the end result of all this preparation. However, as I looked in my full-length mirror before going down, I saw I hadn't turned out badly. There hadn't been time to put up my hair, so I wore it loose with the front held back with a cloisonne butterfly comb. The blue silk dress was sober but at least did emphasize my visible assets.

I felt very unsure before I went down the stairs, very self-conscious when I saw Robin look up. But he seemed pleased, and said, "I like your dress." In his gray suit he didn't seem like the companionable person who'd drunk my wine, or the college professor I'd pelvically lusted after at the restaurant, but more like the fairly famous writer he really was.

We discussed the Pettigrue murder at our table at the Carriage House, where the hostess seemed to recognize Robin's name vaguely. Though maybe she was thinking of the book character. She pronounced it "Cur-so" and gave us a good table.

I asked him to tell me about his job at the university and how it would jibe with his writing time, both questions he seemed to have answered before. I realized this man was used to being interviewed, used to being recognized. I only felt better when I recalled that Lizanne had "bequeathed" him to me, and right on the tail of that thought, Lizanne's parents, Arnie and Elsa, were seated at the table opposite ours. The Crandalls, who had the townhouse to the right of mine, sat down with them.

I had a social obligation here, so I identified them to Robin and went over to their table.

Arnie Buckley jumped right up, and pumped Robin's hand enthusiastically. "Our Lizanne told us all about you!" he said. "We're proud a famous writer like you has come to live in Lawrenceton. Do you like it?" Mr. Buckley had always been a Chamber of Commerce member and unashamed Lawrenceton booster.

"It's an exciting place," said Robin honestly.

"Well, well, you'll have to come by the library. Not as sophisticated as what you'll find in the city, but we like it! Elsa and I are both volunteers. Get to give our time to something now that we're retired!"

"I mostly just help with the book sale," Elsa said modestly.

Elsa was Lizanne's stepmother, but she had been as pretty as Lizanne's mother must have been. Arnie Buckley was a lucky man when it came to pretty women. Now gray-haired and wrinkled, Elsa was still pleasant to look at and be with.

I hadn't known the Buckleys were friends of the Crandalls, but I could see where the attraction would lie. Jed Crandall, like Mr. Buckley, was no chair-bound retiree, but a pepper pot of a man, easily angered and easily appeased. His wife had always been called Teentsy, and was still, though now she certainly outweighed her husband by forty pounds or more.

Teentsy and Jed now said the proper things to Robin about their being neighbors, asking him to drop in, Teentsy saying since he was a poor bachelor (and here she shot me a sly look) he might run short of food sometime, and if he did, just to knock on their door, they had a-plenty, as he could look at her and tell!

"Are you at all interested in guns?" Jed asked eagerly.

"Mr. Jed has quite a collection," I told Robin hastily, thinking he might need to be forewarned.

"Well, sometimes, from a professional standpoint. I'm a mystery writer," he explained when the Crandalls looked blank, though the Buckleys were nodding with vigor, bless their hearts.

"Come by then, don't be a stranger!" Jed Crandall urged.

"Thank you, nice meeting you," Robin said to the table in general, and in a chorus of "see you soon's" and "nice to've met you's" we retired to our table.

The meeting nudged Robin's voracious curiosity, and in telling him about the Crandalls and the Buckleys I began to feel more comfortable. We talked about Robin's new job, and then our food came, and by the time we began eating, I was ready to talk about the murders.

"Jane Engle came by the library today with a pretty solid theory," I began, and told Robin about the likeness of "our" case to that of Cordelia Botkin. He was intrigued.

"I've never heard of anything quite like this," he said after our salad had been served. "What a book this would make! Maybe I'll write about it myself, my first nonfiction book." He had more distance from the case; new in town, he didn't know the victims personally (unless you could term Mother a victim) and probably he didn't know the perpetrator either. I was surprised that the crimes were so exciting to him, until he said after he'd swallowed a mouthful of tomato, "You know, Roe, writing about crime doesn't mean you have direct experience. This is the closest I've ever come to a real murder."

I could have said the same thing as a reader. I'd been an avid fan of both real and fictional crime for years, but this was my closest brush with violent death.

"I hope I never come any closer," I said abruptly.

He reached across the table and took my hand. "It doesn't seem too likely," he said cautiously. "I know the poisoned candy—well, we don't know yet if it was really poisoned or not, do we? That was scarey. But it was impersonal, too, wasn't it? Your mother's situation vaguely fit the Botkin case, even if not as well as Mamie Wright fit Julia Wallace's profile. That was why she was picked."

"But it was sent to *my address*," I said, suddenly letting a fear overwhelm me that I thought I'd suppressed. "That was to involve me. My mother fit the pattern; though that wouldn't have been any consolation to me if she'd died," I added sharply. "But sending it to my place. That was a deliberate attempt to make me—die. Or at least a witness to my mother's dying, or getting sick, depending on what was in the chocolates. That doesn't fit any pattern. That's about as personal as you can get."

"What kind of person could *do* that?" Robin asked.

I met his eyes. "That's the core, isn't it," I said. "That's one reason we like old murders so much. At a safe remove, we can think about the kind of person who can 'do that' without remorse. Almost anyone could kill another person. I guess I could, if it came to being cornered. But I'm sure, I have to be sure, that not many people could sit back and plan other people dying as part of a game the killer decided to play. I have to believe that."

"I do too," he said.

"This really is someone who isn't acting for any of the famous motives Tennyson Jessie wrote about," I continued. "It must be someone acting out something he's always wanted to do. For some reason, now he's able to actually do it."

"A member of your club."

"A former member," I said sadly, and told Robin about the Sunday night meeting.

We had to talk about something else; didn't we have anything to discuss besides murders? Robin, bless him, seemed to see I couldn't take any more, and began telling me about his agent, and about the process of getting a book published. He kept me laughing with anecdotes about book-signings he'd endured and I responded with stories about people that came to the library and some of the wilder questions they'd asked. We actually had a cheerful evening, and we were still at our table when the Crandalls and the Buckleys paid their bill and left.

Since the Carriage House was at the south end of town, we had to pass in front of our townhouses to turn into the driveway on the side. There was a man standing in front of the row of townhouses, on the sidewalk. As we went by, he turned his white face to us and by the light of the streetlamp, I thought I recognized Perry.

I was distracted though by the kiss Robin gave me at my back door. It was unexpected and delicious, and the disparity in our heights was overcome quite satisfactorily. Maybe his asking me out hadn't been quite so impersonal as I'd supposed; his side of the kiss was delivered with great enthusiasm.

I went upstairs humming to myself and feeling very attractive; and when I slipped into my dark bedroom and peered out the window, the street was empty.

THAT NIGHT IT RAINED. I was wakened by the drops pelting against my window. I could see the lightning flicker through my curtains.

I crept downstairs and rechecked my locks. I listened, and heard only the rain. I looked out all the windows and saw only the rain. By the streetlamp out front, I saw the water racing down the slight slope to the storm drain at the end of the block. Nothing else stirred.

ELEVEN

GETTING UP AND GOING to work the next morning wasn't too easy, but it was reassuring. I caught myself humming in the shower and I put on more eye shadow than usual, but my denim skirt, striped blouse, and braided hair felt like a comforting uniform. Lillian and I were mending books in a windowless back room all morning. We managed to get along by swapping recipes or discussing the academic prowess of Lillian's seven-year-old. Though my part of this discussion consisted only of saying "Oh, my goodness," or "Ooh," at the appropriate moments, that suited me. I might have children myself one day—maybe stocky blond ones? Or big-nosed giants with flaming hair? And I would certainly tell everyone I met how wonderful they were.

It was good to get up from the work table and stretch before going home for lunch. I'd been so slow getting up I'd had a scanty breakfast, so I was pretty hungry and trying to visualize what was in my refrigerator as I twisted my key in the lock. When a voice boomed out from behind me, I wasn't frightened, just aggravated that I wasn't going to get to eat.

"Roe! Teentsy said you'd be coming in about now! Listen, we got a little problem in our place," old Mr. Crandall was saying.

I turned around, resigned to postponing food. "What's the little problem, Mr. Crandall?"

Mr. Crandall was not eloquent about anything but guns, and finally I realized that if I was to understand the problem Teentsy was having with the washer, I'd better go along with him.

It wasn't right to feel put-upon; after all, this was my job. But I had been looking forward to eating without Lillian's voice droning in my ears, and since it was Wednesday, there should be a new *Time* in my mailbox. I sighed quietly, and trudged across the patio in Mr. Crandall's wake.

The Crandalls' washer and dryer were in the basement, of course, as they were in all four units. There was a straight flight of rather steep stairs down to the basement, open on one side except for a railing. I clopped down the Crandall's stairs, Teentsy Crandall right behind me telling me about the washer catastrophe in minute detail. When I reached the bottom, I saw a spreading water stain. With a sinking feeling of doom and dismay, I knew I'd have to spend my lunch hour tracking down a plumber.

Despite all the odds against it, I struck gold with my first phone call. The Crandalls watched admiringly as I talked Ace Plumbing into paying my tenants a call in the next hour. Since Ace was one of the two plumbing firms my mother used for all her properties, perhaps it wasn't totally amazing to find them willing; but to actually get them to commit themselves to coming right away—now that was amazing! When I was off the phone and Teentsy put a plate with country fried steak, potatoes, and green beans in front of me, I suddenly saw the bright side of being a resident manager. "Oh, you don't need to do that," I said weakly, and dug in. Calories and cholesterol did not factor in Teentsy's cooking, so her food was absolutely delicious with that added spice of guilt.

Teentsy and Jed Crandall seemed delighted to have someone to talk to. They were quite a pair, Teentsy with her bountiful bosom and childish voice and gray curls, and Jed with his hard-as-a-rock seamed face.

While I ate, Teentsy frosted a cake and Mr. Crandall—I couldn't bring myself to call him Jed—talked about his farm, which he'd sold the year before, and about how convenient it was for them to live in town where all their doctors and kinfolk and grandchildren were. He sounded unconvinced though, and I could tell he was spoiling for something to do.

"That sure was a nice young man we saw you with last night," Teentsy said archly. "Did you two have a good time?"

I was willing to bet Teentsy knew exactly when Robin had brought me home. "Oh, yes, it was fine," I said in as noncommittal a voice as I could summon.

I glanced around their den and kitchen area. Mine was lined with books; Mr. Crandall's was lined with guns. I knew next to nothing about firearms, and was fervently content to keep it that way, but even I could tell these guns were of all different ages and types. I started wondering about their value, and from there it was a natural leap to being concerned about my mother's insurance coverage of these units; what would her responsibility be in case of theft, for example? Though it would take a foolhardy burglar to attempt to take anything away from Jed Crandall.

Thinking of hazards and security in general led my thoughts in another direction. I looked at the Crandalls' back door. Sure enough, they'd added two extra locks.

I laid down my fork. "Mr. Jed, I have to talk to you about those extra locks," I said gently.

Yes, he *had* read his lease agreement carefully. His tough old face went sheepish in an instant.

"Oh, Jed," chided Teentsy, "I told you you needed to speak to Roe about those locks."

"Well, Roe," her husband said, "you can see this gun collection needs more protection than one lock on the back door."

"I can appreciate how you feel, and I even agree," I said carefully, "but you know that if you do put on extra locks, you must give me a key, and you have to leave the locks in and give me all the keys if you ever decide to move. Of course I hope you never will, but you do have to give me an extra set of keys now."

While Mr. Crandall grumbled on about a man's home being his castle, and it going against the grain to give anyone else keys to that castle—even a nice gal like me—Teentsy was on her feet and rummaging through a drawer in the kitchen. She came up with a handful of keys immediately, and began sorting through them with a troubled look on her face.

"Now I've been promising myself I'd go through these and throw away the old ones we didn't need, and since we're retired I should have all the time in the world, but still I haven't done it," she told me. "Well, here are two that I'm sure are the spares for these locks... here, Jed, try them and make sure."

While her husband tested the keys in the locks, she stirred the others around with a helpless finger. "That looks like the key to that old trunk... I don't know about this one... you know, Roe, now that I think about it, one of these keys is to that apartment next door that that Mr. Waites rents now. I know you remember Edith Warnstein, she had it before him. She gave us an extra key because she said she was always locking herself out and it was always when you were at work.''

''Well, when you find it, just bring it over some-time,'' I said. Mr. Crandall handed me his extra keys, which had proved to be the right ones, and I thanked Teentsy for the delicious lunch, feeling even more guilty that they'd fed me and then I'd ''invaded their castle.'' It was hell being conscientious, sometimes. I felt much better when my departure coincided with the arrival of the plumber. Judging solely by his appear-ance—two-day beard stubble, bandanna over long ringlets of black hair, and Day-Glo overalls—I wouldn't have trusted him with *my* washer, but he hefted his tool bag in an authoritative way and actu-ally wrote it down when I told him to bill my moth-er's company for the repairs, so I left feeling I'd performed a service.

I almost literally ran into Bankston on my way out the Crandalls' patio gate. He was hefting his golf bag, and looked shining clean, right out of the shower. He'd obviously been out at the country club having a few rounds. He looked surprised to see me. ''The Crandalls having plumbing problems?'' he asked, nodding towards the plumber's truck.

''Yes,'' I said distractedly, after glancing at my watch. ''Your washer and dryer okay?''

''Oh, sure. Listen, how are you doing after your troubles of the past few days?''

Bankston was being nice and polite, but I didn't have the time or the inclination to chitchat.

"Pretty well, thanks. I was glad to hear that you and Melanie are getting married," I added, remembering that I did owe something to courtesy. "I didn't have the chance to say anything the other night when we met at my place. Congratulations."

"Thanks, Roe," he said, in his deliberate way. "We were lucky to finally really get to know each other." His clear eyes were glowing, and it was apparent to me that he returned Melanie's strong feeling. I was a little envious, to tell the truth, and bitchily wondered what two such stolid people could have to "really get to know." I was also late.

"Congratulations," I repeated sunnily, and pretty much meant it. "I've got to run." I rabbited away to my place to put the keys to the Crandalls' apartment on my official key ring, and though I needed to hurry back to the library, I took an extra minute to label them.

I would've been late anyway.

I DROVE NORTH on Parson Road to get back to the library. The Buckleys' house was along the way, to my left.

By sheer coincidence, out of all the people who could have been driving by when Lizanne came out that front door, it was I. I just glanced to my left to admire the flowers in the Buckleys' front yard, and the front door opened, and a figure stumbled out. I knew it was Lizanne by the color of her hair and her figure and because her parents owned the house, but nothing about her posture and attitude was like Lizanne. She slumped on the front doorstep, clinging to the black iron railing that ran down the red-brick steps.

God forgive me, half of me wanted to continue on my route to the library and go back to work, in blessed ignorance; but the half that said my friend needed help seemed to control the car. I pulled in and crossed the street and then the lawn, dreading to reach Lizanne and find out why her face was so contorted and why there were stains on her hose, especially at the knees.

She didn't know I was there. Her long fingers with their beautifully manicured nails were ripping at her skirt, and her breath tore in and out of her lungs with a horrible wheeze. There were tear stains on her face, though no tears were coming now. From her smell she had vomited recently. The slow, sweet, casual beauty had vanished.

I put my arm around her and tried to forget the sour smell, but it made my own stomach begin to lurch uneasily. The Crandalls' delicious lunch threatened to come right back up. I shut my eyes for a second. When I opened them she was looking at me and her fingers were clenched instead of restless.

"They're both dead, Roe," she said clearly and terribly. "My mama and my daddy are both dead. I knelt down to make sure, and I have my own daddy's blood on my clothes."

Then she fell silent and stared at her skirt, and knowing I was inadequate, could not rise to this ghastly situation, I let my thoughts trace what they were good at: the pattern, the terrible impersonal pattern that real people were being forced to fit. This time it was Lizanne plus dead stepmother and father plus broad daylight plus bloody demise.

I wondered where the hatchet was.

"I just walked to the back door to eat lunch with them like I do every day," she said suddenly. "And when the door was locked, and they wouldn't answer, I unlocked the front here—this is the only key I have. They were—there was blood on the walls."

"The walls?" I murmured stupidly, having no idea what I was going to say until it came out.

"Yes," she said seriously, asserting an incredible truth, "the *walls*. Daddy is on the sofa in there, Roe, the one where he sits to watch television, and he's just all... he's... and Mama is upstairs in the guest bedroom on the floor by the bed."

I held her as tightly as I could and she bent and clung to me.

"I shouldn't have had to see them like that," she whispered.

"No."

Then she lapsed into silence.

I had to call the police.

I stood up like an old woman, and I felt like one. I turned to face the door Lizanne had shut behind her, and reached out like someone in a dream and opened it.

There was blood everywhere, sprayed in trails across the wall. Lizanne was right; blood on the walls. And the ceilings. And the television set.

Arnie Buckley was visible from the front door, which opened opposite the doorway into the den. I supposed it was Arnie. It was the right size and was lying in Arnie's house, on his couch. His face had been obliterated.

I WANTED TO SCREAM until someone knocked me out with a good strong shot. Nothing would get me to set one foot further into this house. More than I ever wanted anything, I wanted to walk back across the street, get in my car, and leave without looking back. It seemed I was always opening doors to look at dead people, hacked people, beaten people. I managed to shut this door, this white-painted suburban front door with the brass knocker, and as I plodded across the Buckleys' lawn to the nearest neighbors, I looked longingly at my Chevette.

I couldn't face calling myself, and I can't remember what I said to the lady next door. I only know that I plodded back to sit by Lizanne on the steps.

She spoke once, asking me in bewilderment why her folks had been killed. I told her, honestly, that they'd been killed by the same person who'd killed Mamie Wright. I hoped she wouldn't ask me why it had to be her parents. Her parents had been picked because she had been named Elizabeth, because she was unmarried, because her "Mama" was not really her mama by blood. This was the pattern of Lizanne's life that loosely fit the Fall River, Massachusetts, murders; the murders committed in 1893 in an ugly, inconvenient, atmospherically tense home in a middle-class neighborhood, almost certainly committed by Mr. Andrew Borden's younger daughter, Lizzie.

But I didn't think Lizanne ever heard anything I said, and that's just as well. I kept my arm around her so something human and warm would be there, and the smell continued to sicken me. I continued to do it because it was all I could do.

Jack Burns got out of the squad car that pulled up on the lawn. He actually had a doctor with him, a local surgeon, and I found out later that they'd been having lunch together when the call came. The doctor looked at Lizanne, at me, and hesitated, but Jack Burns stepped around us and gestured his friend into the house. The sergeant of detectives looked inside and then looked down at me with burning eyes. I was not the object of this look, just in its path. But it scorched me, the fury in those dark eyes.

"Don't touch anything! Be careful how you walk!" he ordered the doctor.

"Well, of course, he's dead," came the doctor's voice. "If you just need me to pronounce him dead, I can sure do that."

"Any more?" Burns spat at me. He could see Lizanne wouldn't answer, I suppose.

"She said her stepmother is dead, upstairs," I told him very quietly, though I don't think Lizanne would have heard me if I'd screamed it.

"Upstairs, Doc!" he ordered.

The doctor probably trotted right up, but I wouldn't have gone with him if a gun had been at my head.

"Dead up here, too," he called down the stairs.

"Then get your ass out of there and let us go over this house," Burns said violently.

The doctor trotted out the door and after thinking for a moment, simply walked down the street. He was not about to ask Jack Burns for a ride back to the restaurant. Burns went inside but I could not hear him walking over the wooden floor. He must be standing, looking. At least he pushed the door partly closed behind him so there was something between me and the horror.

Police cars were pulling up behind Burns's, the routine about to begin. Lynn Liggett got out of the first one. She immediately began giving orders to the uniformed men who spilled out of the next car.

"How did you happen to be here?" Lynn asked without any preliminaries.

"Did you call an ambulance yet for Lizanne?" I asked. I was beginning to shake off my lethargy, my odd dreaminess.

"Yes, there's one on the way."

"Okay. I was just driving to work. She came out of the front door like this. She spoke to me a little and then I opened the door and looked in. I went next door to call the police."

Lynn Liggett pushed open the door and looked in. I kept my eyes resolutely forward. Her fair skin took on a greenish tinge and her lips pressed together so hard they whitened.

The ambulance pulled up then, and I was glad to see it, because Lizanne's face was even waxier, and her hands were losing coordination. Her breathing seemed irregular and shallow. She was leaning on me heavily by the time the stretcher came up to the front steps, and she didn't acknowledge the presence of the ambulance drivers. They loaded her on the stretcher with quick efficiency. I walked by her down to the street, holding her hand, but she didn't know I was there, and by the time the stretcher was pushed into the back of the ambulance she seemed unconscious.

I watched the orange and white ambulance pull away from the curb. I didn't suppose I could leave. I rested on the hood of Lynn's car for what seemed like a long time, staring aimlessly ahead and thinking of as little as possible. Then I became aware Lynn Liggett was beside me.

"There's no question of Lizanne being blamed, is there?" I asked finally. I fully expected the detective to tell me to get lost and it was none of my business, but something had mellowed the woman since last I'd seen her. We had shared something terrible.

"No," Detective Liggett said. "Her neighbor says she heard Lizanne hammer on the back door and then she saw her walk around to the front and unlock the house, something so unusual that the neighbor already considered calling the police. It would take more than seven minutes to do that and clean up afterward. And it's fairly easy to see that her folks had already been dead about an hour by the time she got there."

"Mr. Buckley was due to come in to work at the library today at 2:00, and we were going to share night duty tomorrow night," I said.

"Yes, it's written on the calendar in the kitchen in the house."

For some reason that gave me the cold shudders. Her job included looking at dead people's calendars while they lay right there in their own blood. Appointments that would never be kept. I revised my attitude about Lynn Liggett right then and there.

"You know what this is just like."

"The Borden case."

I jerked my head around to look at her in surprise.

"Arthur's inside," she explained. "He told me about it."

Arthur came out of the house then, with that same whitey-green pinched look Liggett had had. He nodded at me, not questioning my presence.

"John Queensland—from Real Murders?" I said. Arthur nodded. "Well, he's a Borden expert."

"I remembered. I'll get in touch with him this afternoon."

I thought about the sweet old couple I'd seen having a good time at the restaurant the night before. I thought about having to tell the Crandalls their best friends had been hacked to death. Then I realized I should tell the detectives where I'd seen the Buckleys last night, in case for some reason it was important. After I'd explained to Arthur and Lynn, and Lynn had written down the Crandalls' names and the time I'd seen them the previous evening, I wanted to reach over to Arthur, pat or hug him, establish warm living contact with him. But I couldn't.

"It's the worst thing I hope I ever see. They really don't look much like people anymore," Arthur said suddenly. He shoved his hands in his pockets. It was up to his fellow detectives to help him over this one, I realized. I was excluded from this bad moment, and truly, I was thankful.

I thought of a lot of things to say, but they were futile things. It was time for me to go. I got in my car and without considering what I was doing, I drove to work. I went to tell Mr. Clerrick that our volunteer wouldn't be coming in that afternoon.

The rest of the afternoon just passed. Later, I couldn't remember a single thing I'd done after I returned to work. I remembered I'd felt good when I'd gotten up that morning and I couldn't believe it. I just wanted one day with nothing happening, nothing bad, nothing good. No excitement. Just a nice dull day like I'd had almost every day until recently.

Close to closing time, I saw one of the detectives whom I didn't know personally coming into the library. He went to Sam Clerrick's office on the ground floor, emerged in a matter of moments, and made a beeline to Lillian as she stood behind the circulation desk. The detective asked Lillian a couple of questions, and she answered eagerly. He wrote a few things down on his notepad, and left with a nod to her.

Lillian looked up to the second floor where I was again shelving books, and our eyes met. She looked excited, and more than that, turning quickly away. Soon when another librarian was in earshot, Lillian called her over. Their heads tilted close together, and after that the other librarian hurried to the periodicals room, where yet another librarian would be stationed. If the police kept coming here asking about me, I realized with a sick feeling, Mr. Clerrick might let me go. I could tell myself I'd done nothing, but I suddenly knew it wouldn't make any difference. This wasn't just happening to me, I reminded myself. Probably members of Real Murders all over Lawrenceton were being similarly inconvenienced, and many other people whose lives these murders had touched, no matter how tangentially.

It was the old stone-in-the-pond effect. Instead of stones, bodies were being thrown into the pool of the community, and the resulting waves of misery, fear, and suspicion would brush more and more people until the crimes came to an end.

TWELVE

THOUGH I DIDN'T KNOW it until I left work, that afternoon had been a busy one for the news media, as well as the police.

Mamie's death had not aroused much interest in the city, though it had been front-page news in Lawrenceton. The box of candy had rated a couple of paragraphs on an inside page locally, and had failed to register at all in the city. But the murder of Morrison Pettigrue was news; the strange and off-beat murder of a strange and off-beat man, spiced with Benjamin's charge of political assassination. Benjamin may have been a local butcher who very obviously desired attention of any kind in the worst way, but he did deserve the title "campaign manager" and he was quotable. The two local stringers for the city papers enjoyed a couple of days of unprecedented importance.

As Sally had told us so indignantly at the meeting at my place, she'd been asked by the police to keep the Julia Wallace speculations out of the paper. An account of the Julia Wallace murder would have little appeal for twentieth-century American newspaper readers, the police told Sally and her boss. And it would hinder their investigation. Sally was on an inside track with the Wright murder, no doubt about it, being a club member and actually present when the body was found, so she was furious to see her exclusive knowledge stay exclusive. But her boss, Macon Turner, agreed with the local police chief that it should be withheld for "a few days." It was from Macon Turner I pieced all this together later; he'd been wooing my mother for some months before John Queensland gained ascendancy, and we'd become friends.

Sally became frantic after the Pettigrue murder; the minute she'd learned from her police sources that there had been paper scattered on the surface of the bathwater, and that Pettigrue had been placed in the tub after death, she mentally scrolled through the assassinations of radicals and easily came up with the Charlotte Corday's stabbing of Jean-Paul Marat in revolutionary France. Corday had gained entrance to Marat's house by pretending she would give him a list of traitors in her province. Then she killed Marat while he sat in the bath to alleviate a skin disease.

After Sally had thought it through, she exploded into Macon Turner's office and demanded to report the full story. She knew it would be the biggest story of her career. Turner, a friend of the police chief, hesitated a fatal couple of days. Then the Buckleys were slaughtered, and Sally, instantly drawing the obvious conclusion, prepared her story with full disclosure of the "parallel" theory, as it became called.

Turner could no longer resist the biggest, best story that had come along since he'd bought the Lawrenceton *Sentinel.* By chance, the two stringers were not acquainted with any Real Murders members, who at any rate had not been doing a lot of talking about Mamie Wright's murder especially since the Sunday night meeting at my apartment. For example, Le-Master Cane told me later he'd decided even before the meeting that the murders in Lawrenceton were too much like old murders for it to be coincidental. But as a black man, he'd been too scared of being implicated to come forward. He'd already found by that time, too, that his hammer—with initials burned into the haft—was missing. He figured it had been used to kill Mamie.

The same afternoon the Buckleys were found slaughtered, the state lab phoned the local police to say that though the report was in the mail, they wanted Arthur and Lynn to know that what was in the candy my mother had received was a product called "Rat-kill." If my mother had swallowed the candy without noticing the taste in time to spit it out, she would have been very sick. If by some wild chance her tastebuds had been jaded enough for her to eat three choco-lates, she might have died. But the Ratkill had a strong odor and flavor by design, to prevent just such a thing happening; so the poisoning attempt seemed half-hearted and amateurish.

Then Lynn Liggett found the open box of Ratkill in Arthur's car.

The officer who had taken the telephone message from the state crime lab to relay to the detectives was a man named Paul Allison, and he was the brother of the man Sally'd been married to years before. He was a friend of Sally's, and he didn't care for Arthur. Paul Allison was standing in the police station parking lot when Lynn, reaching in Arthur's car to retrieve her forgotten notebook, found an open box of Ratkill under it. Lynn assumed that Arthur had gotten a sample for some reason, and lifted it up where Paul Allison could see it, before she sensed something was wrong and instinctively tried to conceal it.

After Paul Allison had seen the Ratkill, there was no possible way to conceal its finding, and Arthur had a lot of explaining to do; so did Lynn, who had been riding with Arthur off and on.

Paul Allison decided to do his own explaining—to Sally. He called her an hour later, and her full story was in print the next morning.

Sally's story created a sensation, which it fully deserved. Sally Allison, middle-aged newswoman, had finally gotten the story she'd hankered for all her life, and she went for it, no holds barred.

The stringers had not known about the "parallel theory," but they did know something strange was happening in Lawrenceton, which normally had a very low murder rate. When the Buckleys were killed, one of the stringers was listening to her police band scanner. While the police cars converged on the Buckley house, she was loading her camera. She stopped at the gas station to fill up her car, then drove slowly up Parson until she spotted the house. In front of the house was slumped a tall, lovely woman with blood on her legs, and sitting with her arm around the tall, lovely woman was a little librarian with big round glasses and a grim expression. I had been trying to ignore the heave of my stomach, because Lizanne smelled of vomit.

Her picture of us appeared on the front page of the Metro/State section of the evening city paper. Her sources in the police department had not been silent in the meantime, and the caption read: "Elizabeth Buckley sits stunned on the steps of her parents' home after she discovered their bodies. She is being comforted by Aurora Teagarden, who discovered the body of Mrs. Gerald Wright Friday night."

So that afternoon while I worked in a daze at the library newspeople were watching my apartment and my mother's office. It didn't occur to anyone that I might just go on to work after "comforting" Lizanne. Of course, the paper was not yet out and I had not yet seen the picture, but by the time I got back to my apartment after leaving work, a television news crew was parked in my slot in the parking lot. They'd gotten early wind of the story, and since Lizanne was incommunicado in the hospital and Arthur and Lynn were embroiled in the Ratkill discovery at the police station, my mother and I were among the few remaining targets.

That is, until the news crew spotted Robin, who was arriving home from the university. The newsman was an avid mystery buff who recognized Robin, having read of his stepping in for the stricken writer who'd had the heart attack. The camera was trained on him in a flash, and the newsman came up with some hasty questions. Robin, used to being interviewed, handled it well. He was agreeable, without giving them much information. I saw him that night on the news.

Unfortunately, they weren't looking hard enough at Robin to prevent one of them spotting me when I got home. I might think it my duty to talk to the police, but I didn't have to talk to these people. One of them was holding an early copy of the paper, and as I got hesitantly out of my car, stupidly determined on going into my apartment and taking the longest, hottest bath on record, he held it out to me. He said something, I didn't know what, because I was so appalled at seeing the picture of poor Lizanne I couldn't listen.

I felt surrounded, and I was, though the three men of the news team were in my mind magnified to thirty.

I was just worn out and couldn't deal with it.

"I don't want to say anything," I said nervously, and I could tell the camera was running. The newsman was a looker with a beautiful smile, and I wanted him out of my way more than I'd ever wanted anything. I felt I was teetering dangerously on the brink of hysteria.

Robin decided to rescue me. He loomed up behind them, and motioned me to just walk between them. I wondered for a moment if they'd let me, but they parted and I scuttled by straight for Robin. He wrapped his arm around me and we turned out backs on the news team and headed for the patio gate.

I knew the camera was running still (the mystery novelist and his librarian landlady have adjacent apartments) and I had a flash of sense and a jolt of guts. I swivelled to face the camera.

"This is private property. It belongs to my mother and I am her representative here," I said ominously. "You do not have my permission to be on it. This is against the law." I said that like it was a magic charm. And indeed, it seemed to be. For they did pile in their van, and left! I was incredibly pleased with myself, and I was surprised on looking up to see Robin beaming like a fond daddy.

"Go get 'em, Aurora," he said admiringly.

"I appreciate your sheltering me out there in the parking lot, Robin," I said, "but dammit, don't you patronize me!" I did a little independent swivelling and got in my back door without bursting into tears.

That night Arthur called me, to tell me the gloomy story of the Ratkill. "Whoever this asshole is, he's playing games and he just went too far," Arthur said savagely.

I would have thought murdering the Buckleys was going too far, myself.

After I'd commiserated as much as I decently could, I told him about the media problems I was having. I'd gotten several phone calls during my wonderful hot bath, effectively ruining it. Only the chance someone I might want to hear from would call me was keeping me from taking the phone off the hook. For the first time in my life, I was wishing I had an answering machine.

"I'm getting calls, too," Arthur said gloomily. "I'm not used to being the direct subject of all this news attention."

"Neither am I," I said. "I hate it. I'm glad librarians don't have to have press conferences as part of their job. Do you think you're clear now of any suspicion?"

"Yes, I'm not on suspension or anything like that. At least I've built up enough respect here for that."

"I'm glad." And I was. I felt like I had someone on my side in the police force as long as Arthur was there. If he'd been suspended, not only would I have felt bad for his sake, I would have felt powerless.

"Go on and take the phone off the hook," Arthur advised me now. "But first call your mom and get her to put a big sign at the entrance to your parking lot that says in great big letters, 'Private Property, Trespassers will be Prosecuted.'"

"Good idea. Thanks."

We said goodnight uneasily. We were both wondering what would happen next, and who it would happen to.

MY MOTHER WOKE her handyman up with a phone call that night and told him she'd pay him triple if he had the sign in the parking lot by 7:00 the next morning. She begged me to leave town, or come to stay with her, until somehow this situation ended. She'd known the Buckleys, and was horrified by the sheer terror they must have experienced before they died; the Buckleys were her age, her acquaintances.

"John had to go in to talk to the police," she said. "If he can help them, that's wonderful, but I hated for him to go. I wish you'd never joined that damn group, Aurora. But there's no point talking about it now. Won't you come stay over here?"

"Are you going to defend me, Mother?" I asked with a weary smile.

"With my last breath," she said simply.

Suddenly I felt my mother was safer if I stayed away from her.

"I'll manage," I told her. "Thanks for taking care of the sign."

THIRTEEN

I HAD A BAD NIGHT.

I dreamed that men with cameras were coming into the bathroom while I was dressing and that one of them was the murderer. I swam up from a deep sleep to find rain was patting lightly against my bedroom window. I slept again.

When finally I woke up groggy I peered out the upstairs windows from behind my curtains to make sure no one was lying in wait for me. All the cars in the parking lot belonged there. No one was parked out front. There was a large unmistakable sign at the entrance to the parking lot. I padded down the stairs to get my coffee, but took it back up to my room. Mug in hand, I watched Robin leave for work in the city. I saw Bankston go out and get his papers, Teentsy's car pulled out. She must have needed something for breakfast, for she was back within ten minutes. The shower the night before had not amounted to much, not like the rain of two nights ago; the little puddles were already gone.

By the time Teentsy returned, I'd worked up enough courage to get my own papers. They were having a screaming field day. There was a picture of Arthur, a picture of Mamie and Gerald at their wedding, a picture of the Buckleys and Lizanne when the Buckleys had celebrated their twenty-fifth wedding anniversary, and a picture of Morrison Pettigrue taken when he'd announced he was running for mayor, with Benjamin beaming in the background like a proud father.

At least no one seemed to believe that Melanie and Arthur were guilty of anything but being the butt of ghastly practical jokes. I wondered where the hatchet that had killed the Buckleys would turn up, or the knife that had killed Morrison Pettigrue. How could the murderer sustain such a frenzy of activity? Surely there must be an enormous output of physical and emotional energy involved. Surely he must stop.

I managed to dab on some makeup so I wouldn't look like I was going to keel over and yanked my hair back into a ponytail. I pulled on a red turtleneck and navy blue skirt and cardigan. I looked like hell on wheels.

My only goal was to get to the library without anyone noticing me, and find out if there was any chance of putting in a normal day's work. To my utter relief, there were no strange cars in the library parking lot. The interest in me seemed to have ebbed. The day began to look possible.

I found out at work that Benjamin Greer had called a press conference that morning to announce another candidate would run for the Communist Party in the

Lawrenceton mayoral election. The candidate proved to be Benjamin himself, who seemed to be the only other Communist resident of Lawrenceton. I didn't believe for a minute that Benjamin had any coherent political philosophy. He was getting as much publicity as he could while the attention of the media was still on our town. I wondered what would happen to Benjamin after the election. Would butchering at the grocery store ever be enough again?

Lillian Schmidt told me about Benjamin, and altogether covered herself with unexpected glory that morning. She worked side by side with me as though nothing at all had happened, with the exception of describing his press conference. I wanted to ask her why she was being so decent, but couldn't think of a way to phrase it that wasn't offensive. (Why are you being nice to me, when we don't like each other much? Why is a tactless person like you suddenly being the soul of tact?)

I was pulling on my sweater to leave for lunch, when Lillian said, "I know you don't have anything to do with this mess, and I don't think it's fair that all this has happened to you. That policeman coming to ask me yesterday if you were really mending books with me all morning—I just decided last night that was ridiculous. Enough is enough."

For once we agreed on something. "Thanks, Lillian," I said.

I felt a little better as I drove home. I took another route so I didn't have to pass the Buckleys' house. Over lunch I watched the news and saw Benjamin having his minutes of fame.

I was off Thursday afternoon since I was scheduled to work Thursday night. I'd been wise to make the effort to go to work in the morning, I found once I was home alone. Though I liked work, usually I liked my time off even more. Today was an exception. After I'd changed into jeans and sneakers, I couldn't settle on any one project. I did a little laundry, a little reading. I tried a new hairdo, but tore it apart before I was half through. Then my hair was tangled, and I had to brush it through so much to get out the snarls that it crackled around my head in a brown cloud of electric waves. I looked like I'd been contacted by Mars.

I called the hospital to see if I could visit Lizanne, but the nurse on her wing said Lizanne was only receiving visits from family. Then I thought of ordering flowers for the funeral, and called Sally Allison at the newspaper to find out when it would be. For the first time, the receptionist at the *Sentinel* asked my name before ringing Sally. She was riding the crest of the story, that was clear.

"What can I do for you, Roe?" she asked briskly. I felt she was only talking to me because I was still semi-newsworthy at the moment. I had been hot yesterday, but I was cooling off. The lack of excitement in Sally's voice was like a shot of adrenaline to me.

"I just wanted to know when the Buckleys' funeral would be, Sally."

"Well, the bodies have gone for autopsy, and I don't know when they'll be released. So according to Lizanne's aunt, they just haven't been able to make any firm funeral plans yet."

"Oh. Well..."

"Listen, while I've got you on the line...one of the cops said you were on the scene yesterday." I knew Sally had seen the picture of me with Lizanne in the city paper. She was getting too full of herself. "You want to tell me what happened while you were there?" she asked coaxingly. "Is it true that Arnie was dismembered?"

"I wonder if you're really the right person to have on this story, Sally," I said after a long pause during which I thought furiously.

Sally gasped as if her pet sheep had turned and bitten her.

"After all, you're in the club, and I guess we're all really involved, somehow or other, right?" And Sally had a son who was also a member, who could not exactly be called normal.

"I think I can keep my objectivity," Sally said coldly. "And I don't think being a member of Real Murders means you're automatically—involved."

At least she wasn't asking me questions anymore. My doorbell rang.

"I've got to go, Sally," I said gently. And hung up.

I felt mildly ashamed of myself as I went to the door. Sally was doing her job. But I had a hard time accepting her switch from friend to reporter, my changing role from friend to source. It seemed like lately people "doing their jobs" meant I got my life turned around.

I did remember to check my security spy hole. My visitor was Arthur. He looked as ghastly as I had earlier. The lines in his face looked deeper, making him appear at least ten years older.

"Have you had anything to eat?" I asked.

"No," he admitted, after some thought. "Not since five this morning. That's when I got up and went down to the station." I pulled out a chair at my kitchen table and he sat down automatically.

It's hard to perform like Hannah Housewife when you've had no warning, but I microwaved a frozen ham and cheese sandwich, poured some potato chips out of a bag, and scraped together a rather depressing salad. However, Arthur seemed glad to see the plate, and ate it all after a silent prayer.

"Eat in peace," I said and busied myself making coffee and wiping down the kitchen counter. It was an oddly domestic little interval. I felt more myself, less hunted, then I had since stopping to help Lizanne. It was possible work tonight would be entirely normal. And I would come home and sleep, hours and hours, in a clean nightgown.

After he ate, Arthur looked better. When I came to remove his empty plate, he took my wrist and pulled me into his lap, and kissed me. It was long, thorough, and intense. I really liked it very much. But maybe this was a little too fast for me. When by silent mutual accord we unclenched, I wiggled off his lap and tried to slow down my breathing.

"I just wanted to do something I would *enjoy*," he said.

"Quite all right," I said a little unsteadily, and poured him a cup of coffee while gesturing him to the couch. I sat a careful but not marked distance away.

"It's not going well?" I asked tentatively.

"Oh, it's going, now that I've got the Ratkill thing behind me. Of course our fingerprint guy had to go all over my car, and now I've got to get all that stuff off. I'm sure it won't turn up anything. Melanie Clark's car was clean as a whistle. We've completed the Buckley house search, and a neighborhood canvas to see if anyone saw anything. The only thing the house search turned up was a long hair, which may just be one of Lizanne's . . . we have to get a sample from her for comparison. And that's for your ears only. The murder weapon hasn't turned up yet, but it was a hatchet or something like that, of course."

"You're really not a suspect?"

"Well, if I ever was, I'm not now. While the Buckleys were being murdered I was going door to door with another detective asking questions about the Wright murder. And come to think of it, right before the last meeting, when Mamie Wright was done in, I was booking a DWI at the station. I drove to the meeting directly from there. And Lynn was able to swear for me that the Ratkill hadn't been in the car all morning while we were riding around knocking on doors."

"Good," I said. "Someone's got to be out of the running."

"And thank God it's me, since the department needs every warm body it can get on this one. I've got to go." He heaved himself to his feet, looking tired again.

"Arthur...what about me? Does anyone think I did it?"

"No, honey. Not since Pettigrue, anyway. His old house had one of those claw-footed tubs, way off the floor, and he was a tall man, maybe six-three. You couldn't have gotten him in that tub alone, no way. And around Lawrenceton enough people would know if you were steadily seeing some guy who'd help you move the body. No, I think Pettigrue definitely let you off the hook in just about everyone's mind."

It was unnerving to think that my name had been spoken by men and women I didn't know, men and women who seriously considered I might have killed people in brutal and bloody ways. But all in all, after I'd talked to Arthur, I felt much better.

I saw him off with a light squeeze of his hand, and sat down to think a little. It was about time I thought instead of felt. I had crammed more feelings into the past week than I had in a year, I estimated.

The hair the police had found was probably brown, since it might be Lizanne's and hers was a rich chestnut. Who else could have shed that hair?

Well, I was a member of Real Murders who had long brown hair. Luckily for me, I'd been repairing books with Lillian Schmidt all morning. Melanie Clark had medium-length dull brown hair, and Sally, though her hair was shorter and lighter, could also be a contender. (Wouldn't it be something if Sally had committed all these murders so she could report them? A dazzling idea. Then I told myself to get back on the track.) Jane Engle's hair was definitely gray... then I thought of Gifford Doakes, whose hair was long and smoothly moussed into a pageboy or sometimes gathered in a ponytail, to John Queensland's disgust. Gifford was a scarey person, and he was so interested in massacres...and his friend Reynaldo would probably do anything Gifford wanted.

But surely someone as flamboyant as Gifford would have been noticed going into the Buckleys' house?

Well, discarding the possible clue of the hair for the moment, how had the murderer gotten in and left? A neighbor had seen Lizanne enter, too soon before I'd arrived to have done everything that had been done to the Buckleys. So someone was in a position to view the front of the Buckley house at least part of the morning. I considered other approaches and tried to imagine an aerial view of the lot, but I am not good at geography at all, much less aerial geography.

I sat a while longer and thought some more, and found myself wandering to the patio gate several times to see if Robin was home yet from the university. It was going to rain later, and the day was cooling off rapidly. The sky was a dull uniform gray.

I pulled on my jacket finally and was heading out on my own when his big car pulled in. Robin unfolded from it with an armful of papers. Why doesn't he carry a briefcase? I wondered.

"Listen, change your shoes and come with me," I suggested.

He looked down his beaky nose at my feet. "Okay," he said agreeably. "Let me drop these papers inside. Someone stole my briefcase," he said over his shoulder.

I pattered after him. "Here?" I said, startled.

"Well, since I moved to Lawrenceton, and I'm fairly sure from here in the parking lot," he said as he unlocked his back door.

I followed him in. Boxes were everywhere, and the only thing set in order was a computer table suitably laden with computer, disc drives, and printer. Robin dumped the papers and bounded upstairs, returning in a few seconds with some huge sneakers.

"What are we going to do?" he asked as he laced them up.

"I've been thinking. How did the murderer get into the Buckleys' house? It wasn't broken into, right? At least the papers this morning said not. So maybe the Buckleys left it unlocked and the killer just walked in and surprised them, or the killer rang the doorbell and the Buckleys let him—or her—in. But anyway, how did the killer approach the house? I just want to walk up that way and see. It had to be from the back, I think."

"So we're going to see if we can do it ourselves?"

"That's what I thought." But as we were leaving Robin's I had misgivings. "Oh, maybe we better not. What if someone sees us and calls the police?"

"Then we'll just tell them what we're doing," said Robin reasonably, making it sound very simple. Of course, *his* mother wasn't the most prominent real estate dealer in town and a society leader to boot, I reflected.

But I had to go. It had been my idea.

So out of the parking lot we went, Robin striding ahead and me trailing behind, until he looked back and shortened his stride. The parking lot let out in the middle of the street that ran beside Robin's end apartment. Robin had turned right so I did, too, and at the corner we turned north to walk the two blocks up Parson to the Buckleys'. Perhaps as I'd driven past the Buckleys' on my way home to lunch the day before, the Buckleys were being slaughtered. I caught up with Robin at the next corner, shivering inside my light jacket. The house was on this next block.

Robin looked up the street, thinking. I looked down the side street; no houses faced the road. "Of course, the trash alley," I said, disgusted with myself.

"Huh?"

"This is one of the old areas, and this block hasn't been rebuilt in ages," I explained. "There's an alley between the houses facing Parson Road and the houses facing Chestnut, which runs parallel to Parson. The same with this block we're standing on. But when you get south to our block, it's been rebuilt, with our apartments for one thing, and garbage collection is on the street."

Under the gray sky we crossed the side street and came to the alley entrance. I'd felt so pursued and viewed yesterday, it was almost eerie how invisible I felt now. No houses facing this side street, little traffic. When we walked down the gravelled alley, it was easy to see how the murderer had reached the house without being observed.

"And almost all these yards are fenced, which blocks the view of the alley," Robin remarked, "and of the Buckleys' back yard."

The Buckleys' yard was one of the few unfenced ones. The ones on either side had five-foot privacy fences. We stopped at the very back of the yard by the garbage cans, with a clear view of the back door of the house. The yard was planted with the camellias and roses that Mrs. Buckley had loved. In their garbage can—what an eerie thought—was probably a tissue she'd blotted her lipstick with, grounds from the coffee they'd drunk on their last morning, detritus of lives that no longer existed.

Yes, their garbage was surely still there...everyone on Parson Road had garbage pickup on Monday. They'd been killed on Wednesday. I shuddered. "Let's go," I said. My mood had changed. I wasn't Delilah Detective anymore.

Robin turned slowly. "So what would you do?" he said. "If you didn't want to be observed, you'd have parked your car—where? Where we came into the alley?''

"No. That's a narrow street, and someone might remember having to pull out and around to get past your car.''

"What about at the north end of the alley?''

"No. There's a service station right across the street there, it's real busy.''

"So," said Robin, striding ahead purposefully, "we go back this way, the way we came. If you had an ax, where would you put it?''

"Oh, Robin," I said nervously. "Let's just go." We were leaving the alley as unobserved as we had entered, as far as I could tell, and I was glad of it.

"I," continued Robin, "would drop it in one of these garbage cans waiting to be emptied.''

That was why Robin was a very good mystery writer.

"I'm sure the police have searched them," I said firmly. "I am not going to stand here and go through everyone's garbage. Then someone really would call the police." Or would they? Apparently no one had spotted us so far.

We'd reached the end of the alley, at the spot we'd entered.

"If you wouldn't park here, you might just cross the street and go through the next alley," he said thoughtfully. "Park even farther away, be even less likely to be seen and connected."

So we slipped across the narrow street into the next alley. This one had been widened a little when some apartments had been built. Their parking was in the back, and in the construction process a drainage ditch had been put in the alley to keep the parking lots clear. There were culverts to provide entrances and exits to the lots. I thought, I would put the ax in one of the culverts. And I wondered if the police had searched this block.

This alley too was silent and lifeless, and I began to have the unsettling feeling that maybe Robin and I were the only people left in Lawrenceton. The sun came out briefly and Robin took my hand, so I tried hard to feel better. But when he crouched to retie his shoe, I began looking in the ditches.

Certainly the culvert right by us hadn't been disturbed. The water oak leaves that half-blocked the opening were almost smoothly aligned, pointing in the same direction, by the heavy rain of the night before last. But the next one down...someone had been in that ditch, no doubt about it. The leaves had been shoved up around the opening so forcefully that the mud underneath had been uncovered. Perhaps the police had searched, but of course none of them were as short as I was, so they weren't at an angle to see a little gleam from inside the culvert, a gleam sparked by the unexpected and short-lived sunshine. And their arms weren't as long as Robin's so they couldn't have reached in and pulled out . . .

"My briefcase?" Robin said in shock and amazement. "What's it doing here?" His fingers pried the gold-tone locks.

"Don't open it!" I shrieked, as Robin opened it, and out fell a bloodstained hatchet, to land with a thud on the packed leaves in the ditch.

FOURTEEN

WHILE ROBIN STOOD GUARD over the horrible thing in the alley, I knocked on the door of one of the apartments. I could hear a baby screaming inside, so I knew someone was awake.

The exhausted young woman who answered the door was still in her nightgown. She was trusting enough to open the door to a stranger, and tired enough to accept my need to use her telephone incuriously. The baby screamed while I looked up the number of the police station, and kept it up while I dialled and talked to the desk officer, who had some trouble understanding what I was trying to tell him. When I hung up and thanked the young woman, the baby was still crying, though it had ebbed to a whimper.

"Poor baby," I said tentatively.

"It's colic," she explained. "The doctor says the worst should be over soon."

Aside from occasionally babysitting my half-brother Phillip when he was small, I knew nothing about babies. So I was glad to hear that the child had a specific complaint. By the time I thanked her and she shut the door behind me, I could hear the child starting to cry again.

I trudged back to the alley where Robin was sitting glumly, his back propped against the fence on the side opposite the apartments.

"Me and my great ideas," I said bitterly, plopping down beside him.

He let that pass in a gentlemanly manner.

"Cover it up," I suggested. "I can't stand it."

"How, without getting fingerprints on it? More fingerprints, that is."

We solved that problem as a mist began to dampen my hair against my cheeks. I found a stick and Robin stuck it under the edge of the briefcase, lifting it and dragging it over the hatchet with its dreadful stains. We settled back against the fence, able now to hear the sirens approaching. I felt oddly calm.

"I wonder if I'll ever get my briefcase back," Robin said. "Someone came in our parking lot and reached in my car, and took my briefcase, so he could use it for hiding a murder weapon. I'd been thinking, Roe, when this case is all over, if it ever is, that I might try my hand at nonfiction. I'm here, I'm involved through knowing some of the people. I even met the Buckleys the very night before they were killed. I was there when you and your mother opened the chocolates. Now I'm here finding a murder weapon in *my* briefcase, and I'm telling you, I don't like this much anymore. I don't think I even want the damn briefcase as a memento, now that I think of it." But after sitting for a moment in silence, he murmured, "Wait till I tell my agent."

The surface of his glasses began to be speckled with tiny drops of moisture. I took my own off and wiped them with a Kleenex. "I've got to admire your lack of fear, Robin," I said.

"Lack of fear?"

"You think they're not going to want to ask you a few questions?" I said pointedly.

He had only seconds to absorb this and look dismayed before an unmarked car pulled in the alley, with a patrol car right behind it. For some reason, we stood up.

And God bless me, who should emerge from the unmarked car but my friend Lynn Liggett, and she was mad as a wet hen.

"You're everywhere!" she said to me. "I know you didn't do these murders, but I swear every time I turn around you're right in front of me!" She shook her head, as if trying to shake me out of it. Then words seemed to fail her. Her glance fell on the overturned open briefcase, with the handle of the hatchet protruding slightly from underneath.

"Who covered it up?" she said next. After we told her, and she lifted the briefcase from the bloody hatchet with the same stick, all her attention was on the murder weapon.

Yet another car appeared behind the patrol car. My heart sank even deeper as Jack Burns heaved himself out and strolled towards us. His body language said he was out for a casual amble in a pleasant neighborhood but his dark eyes snapped with anger and menace.

He stopped at the patrolmen, apparently the ones who had conducted the original alley search the day before and blistered them up and down in language I had only seen in print. Robin and I watched with interest as they began to search the alley for anything that might have been left by the murderer. I was willing to bet that if he'd left any other trace in the alley, this time it would be found.

People began to emerge from the apartments, and the alley that had seemed so silent and deserted began to be positively crowded. I saw the curtain move at the apartment of the young mother, and hoped the baby had calmed down by now. It occurred to me that this woman was the most likely to have seen something the previous day, since she was probably up almost all the time. I started to suggest this to Detective Liggett, but I reconsidered in time to save my head from being bitten off.

The hatchet and briefcase bagged, the policewoman turned back to us.

"Did you touch the briefcase, Miss Teagarden?" she asked me directly.

I shook my head.

"So you did," she said to Robin, who nodded meekly. "You're someone else who turns up everywhere."

Finally Robin began to look worried.

"You need to go down to the station and have your fingerprints taken," Lynn said brusquely.

"I had them made the other night," Robin reminded her. "Everyone at the Real Murders meeting had his or her prints taken."

This reminder did not endear him to the detective.

"Whose idea was this stroll through the alley?" Lynn counterattacked.

We looked at each other.

"Well," I began, "I started wondering how the Buckleys' murderer had reached their house without being seen . . ."

"But it was definitely me that wanted to go through this alley as well as the one behind the Buckley house," Robin said manfully.

"Listen, you two," Lynn said with an assumed calm, "you don't seem to understand the real world very well."

Robin and I didn't care for that accusation. I felt him stiffen beside me, and I drew myself up and narrowed my eyes.

"We are the police, and *we* are paid too damn little to investigate murders, but that's what we do. We don't sit and read about them, we solve them. We find clues, and we track down leads, and we knock on doors." She paused and took a deep breath. I had found several flaws in her speech so far, but I wasn't about to point out to her that Arthur read a lot about murders and that the police so far hadn't solved a thing and that the clue of the hatchet would still be in the damn ditch if Robin and I hadn't unearthed it.

I had enough sense of self-preservation not to say those things. When Robin cleared his throat, I stepped on his toes.

I was sorry I'd stopped him a moment later when Lynn really began questioning him. I wouldn't have stood to her questioning as well as he, and I had to admire his composure. I could see that it did look peculiar; Robin arrives in town, the murders start. But I knew that Mamie Wright's murder had been planned before Robin came to live in Lawrenceton, and the chocolates had been sent to Mother even earlier. The officer pointed out, though, that Robin had been present at the discovery of Mamie Wright's body, having invited himself to a Real Murders meeting on his first night in town. And he'd been at my house when I'd received the chocolate box.

Lynn was certainly not the only detective who thought Robin's presence at so many key scenes was fishy. And perhaps I was not as clear and free of suspicion as Arthur had assured me, because when Jack Burns took up the questioning he was looking from Robin to me with some significance. Here, he seemed to be thinking, is someone big who could have helped this woman get Pettigrue's body in the bathtub.

"I have to go to work in an hour and a half," I said quietly to him, when I'd had all I could take.

He stopped in mid-sentence.

"Sure," he said, seeming abruptly exhausted. "Sure you do." His fuel, it seemed, had been his exasperation with his own men missing the hatchet, and he'd run out of it. I liked him a lot better all of a sudden.

When Burns had taken over the role of castigator, Lynn had started knocking door to door at the apartments asking questions. Finally she reached the apartment where I'd used the phone, and the young woman, now in jeans and a sweater—she'd undoubtedly seen the police going door to door—answered in a flash. Lynn was obviously running through her list of questions, but I noticed after about the third one, she came to point like a bird dog. The young woman had said something Lynn was interested in hearing.

"Jack," Lynn yelled, "come here."

"Go home," Burns told us simply. "We know where you are if we need you." And he hurried over to Lynn.

Robin and I blew out a breath of relief simultaneously, and almost slunk out of the alley, trying as hard as we possibly could to attract no more official attention. Once we were out into the street, Robin went flying along home and dragged me with him by the hand.

When we reached our parking lot we finally stopped for breath. Robin hugged me and dropped a quick kiss on the top of my head, the most convenient spot for him. "That was really interesting," he commented, and I began laughing until my sides hurt. Robin's red eyebrows flew up, and his glasses slid down, and then he began laughing, too. I looked at my watch while I was thinking how long it had been since I'd really whooped like that, and when I saw what the time was, I told Robin I had to go change clothes. At least for a few hours, I had forgotten to be afraid about working at the library alone that night.

It had not been noticed until the last moment that no one had been scheduled to take Mr. Buckley's place on the roster. None of the other librarians would now admit to having the evening free, and all the volunteers had been scheduled for other nights.

I told Robin this hurriedly, and he said, "I'm sure the police patrols have been stepped up. But maybe I'll stop in on you tonight. If you need me, call me. I'll be here." He went in his gate and I went in mine.

As I pulled on the same blue skirt and red turtleneck I'd worn that morning, I was doing my best not to think of the hatchet. It had been unspeakable. On my drive to work I hoped that the library would be flooded with patrons so I wouldn't have time to think.

I was taking over the checkout desk from Jane Engle, who had been substituting for one of the librarians whose child had the flu. Jane looked the same, with her perfectly neat gray hair, her perfectly clean wire-rimmed glasses, and her anonymous gray suit. But inside, I could see she was no longer a sophisticated and curious witness to the Lawrenceton murders, but a terrified woman. And she was glad to get out of the library. "All the others left at five, not a single patron's come in since then," she told me in a shaky voice. "And frankly, Aurora, I've been delighted. I'm scared to be alone with anyone anymore, no matter how well I think I know them."

I patted Jane on the arm awkwardly. Though at times we'd eaten lunch together, mostly on days after club meetings when we wanted to discuss the program, Jane and I had had a friendly, but never intimate, relationship.

"Other people are interested in our little club for the first time," Jane went on, "and I've had to answer a lot of questions no one ever bothered to ask me before. People think I'm a little strange for having belonged to Real Murders." Jane was definitely a woman who would hate to be thought strange.

"Well," I said hesitantly, "just because we had a different sort of hobby—." Come to think of it, maybe we *were* a little strange, all of us Real Murderers, as we had sometimes called ourselves laughingly. Ho-ho.

"One of us really is a murderer, you know," Jane chimed in eerily. I felt my thoughts were becoming visible in a balloon over my head. "It's gone beyond an academic interest in death and gore and psychology. I could feel it that night we met in your apartment."

"Whom do you think it is, Jane?" I said impulsively, as she tied her scarf and extracted her keys from her purse.

"I am sure it's someone in our club, of course, or possibly a near connection of some sort to a club member. I don't know if this person has always been disturbed, or if he's just now decided to play a ghastly series of tricks on his fellow members. Or maybe there is more than one murderer and they're acting together."

"It doesn't have to be someone in Real Murders, Jane, just someone who doesn't like one of us, someone who wants us to be in trouble." She was standing by the front door by then, and I wanted her to stay as much as she wanted to go.

She shrugged, not willing to argue. "It's frightening to me," she said quietly, "to imagine what case I fit. I go over my books, checking out cases, to see what elderly woman living alone I resemble. What old murder victim."

I stared at her with my mouth open. I was appalled to realize what Jane had been going through, because of her active and probably accurate mind.

Then a mother trailing two reluctant toddlers came through the door, and Jane slipped out to go home to her waiting house, to leaf through her true crime books in search of the pattern she would fit.

THANK GOD OTHER people were in the library when Gifford Doakes came in, or I might have shrieked and run. Gifford, massacre enthusiast, had always sounded the warning bell in my brain that cautions me to pick and choose my conversation topics. Though I really didn't know too much about him, I'd always kept my distance from Gifford and limited my contact with him to the bare bones of courtesy.

You wanted to be polite to Gifford. You were a little scared not to be.

I had no idea what Gifford did for a living, but he dressed like a "Miami Vice" drug lord, in extremely stylish clothes and with his long brown hair carefully arranged. I wouldn't have been surprised to see a shoulder holster under his jacket.

Maybe Gifford *was* a drug lord.

And here he came now, gliding over to the checkout desk. I glanced around; that dynamic twosome, Melanie Clark and Bankston Waites, had come in a few minutes previously, their heads close together and laughing, and I could now see Bankston upstairs in the biography section, while Melanie was flipping through *Good Housekeeping* in the magazine area on the ground floor. Probably looking for a new meatloaf recipe. But bless her, she was there within call.

Gifford was right across the desk from me, and my hand closed over the nearest thing, which proved to be the stapler. A really effective deterrent, I told myself bitterly. I could see his shadow, Reynaldo, standing outside the double glass doors, pacing around in the near-dark of the parking lot. He would pass through a pool of light from the arc lamps that provided safety for the lot—theoretically—and then vanish into the gloom, reappearing seconds later.

"How ya doing, Roe?" Gifford asked perfunctorily.

"Um. Okay."

"Listen, I hear you and that writer found the murder weapon in the Buckley case today."

The Buckley case? I had a sudden vision of an anthology of accounts of the decade's most notable murders, and of Lizanne's parents' slaughter being included. Other people would read about their deaths, and speculate, as I had speculated about other unsolved cases. Could it have been The Daughter? Or the Policeman who also belonged to the Real Murders Club? I realized that these murders would be made into a book...maybe by Joe McGuinniss or Joan Barthel or Robin, if his taste for it revived...and I would be in it, because of the chocolates. Maybe just "when the candy arrived at the home of Mrs. Teagarden's daughter Aurora...."

For a minute I was very confused. Was I in a book about old murders that I was reading, or was this all happening to me now? It would be nice to have the distance a book would give me. But Gifford's one earring was all too real, and the leopard-like pacing of Reynaldo—in the prosaic library parking lot!—was all too real, too.

"Tell me about the ax," Gifford was demanding.

"It was a hatchet, Gifford. An ax wouldn't fit in a briefcase." I was immediately furious with myself for contradicting a scarey guy like Gifford; but then I consciously realized what my unconscious must have noted. Gifford Doakes was a man with a mission, and he was not interested in sidetracks.

"This long?" He held his hands apart.

"Yes, about." Standard hatchet size.

"Wood handle with black tape wrapped around the grip?"

"Yes," I agreed. I had forgotten the tape until he mentioned it.

"Damn," he hissed, and then he said a few other things, and his dark eyes blinked rapidly. Gifford Doakes was a frightened man and a furious one. I was scared as hell, too, not only of the murderer but more immediately of Gifford. Who was maybe also the murderer.

I gripped the stapler even harder, and felt like a fool planning to battle a crazy man with a stapler that even, I suddenly remembered, contained no staples. Well, strike that line of defense.

"Now I have to go to the police station," Gifford said unexpectedly. "That's my hatchet, I'm almost positive. Reynaldo found out it was missing yesterday."

I laid down the stapler very gently on my desk, glanced upward and saw Bankston looking over the second-floor railing. He raised his eyebrows in a silent query. I shook my head. I didn't think I needed help anymore. I thought Gifford was just as nervous as the rest of us, and for good reason. At this moment, sophisticated pageboy and sharp clothes notwithstanding, Gifford was chewing on his thumbnail like a five-year-old facing a difficult world.

"You'd better go to the police now," I said to him carefully. And he wheeled and was out the door before I could catch my breath.

Gifford's hatchet, Robin's briefcase. Those not cast as victims were being cast as murderers, to provide even more fun for the killer.

I wondered which category was scheduled for me. Surely finder-of-the-body would suffice.

I was still pondering this and other unpleasant related topics thirty minutes later when Perry Allison came in. I could hardly believe my luck at seeing Gifford and Perry in one evening. Two great guys. At least while Gifford had been here, so had a few other people, but in the intervening half hour Bankston and Melanie and the two other patrons had trickled out the door.

This time I quietly opened a drawer and slid out a pair of scissors. I checked my watch; only fifteen minutes to go till closing time.

"Roe!" he babbled. "Qué pasa?" His hands beat a manic tattoo on the desk.

I felt a stirring of dismay. This wasn't even the familiar unpleasant Perry, who had perhaps skipped some prescribed medication. Perry was on drugs no doctor had ever given him. The appeal of "recreational" drugs had completely passed me by, but I wasn't totally naive.

"Nothing much, Perry," I said cautiously.

"How can you say that? Things here are just *hopping*," he told me, his eyebrows flying all over his narrow face. "A murder a day, practically. Your honey, the cop, was at my place this afternoon. Asking questions. Making insinuations. About me! I couldn't hurt a fly!"

And Perry laughed and came around the desk in a few quick steps.

"Scissors?" He whooped. "Sssssscisssssors?" He experimented with hissing. I was so taken aback by his quick moves and jerky head movements, so unlike the Perry I worked with, that it took me by surprise when his hand shot out to grasp the wrist of my hand that was holding the scissors. He gripped with manic pressure.

"That hurts, Perry," I said sharply. "Let go."

But Perry laughed and laughed, never relaxing his grip. I knew in a minute I would drop the scissors and I could not imagine what would happen after that.

Abruptly, he turned enraged. "You were going to stab me," he shouted furiously. "Not one of you wants me to make it! Not one of you knows what that hospital was like!"

He was right, and under other circumstances I would have listened with some sympathy. But I was in pain and terrified.

I could just barely feel the scissors still gripped in my numbing fingers.

In a day filled with strange incidents, this crazed man screaming at me, his emotional intensity spilling over me in this quiet and civilized building where people came to pick out nice quiet civilized books.

Then he began shaking me to get me to listen, his other hand gripping my shoulder like a vise, and he never stopped talking, angry, sad, full of pain and self-pity.

I began to get angry myself, and suddenly something in me just snapped. I raised my foot and stomped on his instep with every ounce of force I could summon. With a wail of pain, he let go of me, and in that instant I turned and raced for the front door.

I ran smack into Sally Allison.

"Oh my God," she said hoarsely. "Are you all right? He didn't hurt you?" Without waiting for an answer she shouted at her son over my head, "Perry, what in God's name has gotten into you?"

"Oh, Mom," he said hopelessly and began to cry.

"He's on drugs, Sally," I said raggedly. She held me away from her and scanned me for injuries, letting loose a visible sigh of relief when she saw no blood. She saw the scissors still in my hand and looked horrified. "You weren't going to hurt him?" she asked incredulously.

"Sally, only a mother could say that," I said. "Now, you get him out of here and take him home."

"Listen to me, please, Roe," Sally pleaded. I was still frightened, but I was acutely uncomfortable, too. I had never had anybody beg me, as Sally unmistakably was begging me now. "Listen, he didn't take his medicine today. He's okay when he takes his medicine, really. You know he can come to work and perform his job, no one's complained about that, right? So please, please don't tell anyone about this.''

"About what?'' asked a quiet voice above my head, and I realized Robin had come in quietly. I looked up to his craggy face, his now-serious crinkly mouth, and I was so glad to see him I could have wept. "I came to check up on you,'' he said to me. "Mrs. Allison, I think I met you at the club meeting.''

"Yes,'' Sally said, trying hard to pull herself together. "Perry! Come on!''

He walked over to her, his wet face blank and tired, his shoulders slumped.

"Let's go home,'' his mother suggested. "We have to talk about our agreement, about the promise you made me.''

Without looking at me or saying a word, Perry followed his mother out the door. I collapsed against Robin and cried a little, still holding the stupid scissors. His huge hand smoothed my hair. When the worst was over, I said, "I have to lock up, I'm closing now. I don't care if Santa Claus comes to check out a book. This library is closed.''

"Going to tell me what happened?''

"You bet I am, but first I want to get out of this place.'' I hated detaching myself from the comfortable chest and enfolding arms; it had been nice to feel protected by a big strong man for a few seconds. But I wanted to leave that building and go home more than I wanted anything else, and with luck, we could repeat the scene at my place with amenities handy.

FIFTEEN

"MAYBE," ROBIN speculated between bites of a pretzel stick, "there's more than one murderer."

If we ever spent a night together, it wasn't going to be tonight. The mood had faded.

"Oh, Robin! I can't believe that for a minute. There couldn't be two people that evil in Lawrenceton at the same time, doing the same thing!" One was bad enough; two would get us in the history books for sure.

He waved the pretzel stick at me emphatically. "Why not, Roe? A copycat killer. Maybe someone, for example, wanted the Buckleys out of the way for some reason, and after Mamie got killed he saw his chance. Or maybe someone wanted to do in Pettigrue, and killed Mamie and the Buckleys to cloud the issue."

There was a certain amount of precedent for that, but more often in mystery novels than in real life, I thought.

"I guess it's possible," I conceded. "But Robin, I just don't want to believe it."

"Maybe, then, there's more than one killer. I mean, a team of murderers."

"Jane Engle said the same thing," I recalled belatedly. "Two people? How could you look at anyone who knew you had done that, Robin?" I could truly not imagine saying, "Hey, buddy, look at the way I socked Mamie!" I felt almost nauseated. That two people could agree on such a plan, and mutually carry it out....

"Hillside Stranglers," Robin reminded me. "Burke and Hare."

"But the Hillside Stranglers were sex murderers," I objected, "and Burke and Hare wanted to sell the bodies to medical schools."

"Well, true. These killings are apparently just for fun. Just to tease."

I thought of Gifford and his hatchet. The killer was teasing in more than one way. "Wait till you hear this!" I exclaimed.

Robin felt better when I'd told him he and Melanie and Arthur had company in the category of Implicated Innocent. "Though it would be clever of this Gifford," Robin cautioned, "to use his own ax, and then claim its use proved him innocent."

"I wonder if Gifford is that clever," I said. "Gifford is crafty, I think, but I believe he's pretty limited in imagination."

"And how well do you know him?" asked Robin, with a tiny edge to his voice.

"Not well," I admitted. "Just through seeing him at Real Murders. He's been coming about a year, I think. And he brings a *friend* named Reynaldo. Who apparently doesn't have a last name..."

The phone rang, and I reached out to pick it up, surprised at getting such a late call. People in Lawrenceton do not make phone calls after 10:00 P.M. At least, not the people I know. Robin tactfully took the occasion to go into the bathroom.

"Oh, God, I just looked at my watch, were you in bed?" Arthur asked.

"No," I said, feeling ridiculously awkward with Robin in my place. Why should I? I asked myself. I could see two men at one time if I chose.

"I just finished work and got back to my place. I don't suppose there's any chance you want to come over?"

The idea sent a certain tingle down my spine, but all the conditions that had applied to Robin were still valid; plus, Robin was showing no signs of budging. In fact, he'd just gone to the refrigerator and refreshed his drink.

"I have to work tomorrow," I said neutrally.

"Oh. Okay. I get the message. Roller skating or nothing."

Ohmygosh. I had almost forgotten. Well, I had some pretty good reasons for not thinking about a Saturday night date.

"You think you will be able to get off?" I asked cautiously.

"I think so. I have some amazing news for you. You sitting down?"

Arthur sounded strange. Like someone who was trying to be excited and happy and just couldn't manage. And he hadn't mentioned the discovery of the hatchet and briefcase.

"Yes, I'm sitting. What?"

"Benjamin Greer just confessed to all the murders."

"What? He what?"

"He confessed to killing Mamie Wright, Morrison Pettigrue, and the Buckleys."

"But what about the box of candy? Why did he do that? Mother doesn't know him at all."

"He says Morrison did that, because your mother is an example of what is worst about capitalism."

"My mom—Morrison Pettigrue? I don't believe it," I sputtered disconnectedly.

"You don't want this case to be over?"

"Yes, yes! But I don't believe he did it. I wish I did."

"He's convinced a lot of the guys down here."

"Did he know where the hatchet was hidden?"

"Everyone in town knows that now."

"Did he know what it was in?"

"Pretty much everyone knows that, too."

"Okay, who'd he steal the hatchet from, that he used to kill the Buckleys?"

"He hasn't said yet."

"Gifford Doakes told me tonight that it was his hatchet."

"He did?" And for the first time Arthur's voice showed some life and enthusiasm. "Gifford hasn't been in here yet. As far as I know."

"Well, he told me tonight at the library that his hatchet had been missing, and he asked me about that tape around the handle. I didn't bring it up, in fact I'd forgotten about it."

"I'll pass that on to the men who are questioning Greer," Arthur promised. "That can be one of our test questions. But for some reason, Roe, this guy is convincing. He believes it, I think. And we have a witness."

Robin had abandoned being polite and was beside himself to know what I was talking about. His eyebrows were winging around his face in interrogation. I kept waving my hand to keep him quiet.

"A witness to the murder."

"No, a witness who saw him leave the hatchet in the alley."

I remembered Lynn's excitement when she'd talked to the young mother in the apartments. I was willing to bet that that was the witness.

"So what did she see?" I asked sharply.

"Listen, this is police business that I can't tell you about in detail," Arthur said flatly.

"I'm sorry if I'm trespassing, but I'm deeply involved in this, up to my neck, according to Lynn Liggett and your boss Jack Burns."

"Well. You're off the hook now."

"This is hard to soak in. I can't believe it's all over."

"I'm going home to sleep," Arthur said, and the exhaustion made his voice slur. "I'm going to sleep and sleep and sleep. And when I get up, we're going to talk about going roller skating."

"Okay," I said slowly. "Listen, I just remembered that my little brother Phillip is coming tomorrow and spending the weekend."

"Then we'll take him with us," Arthur said smoothly, scarcely missing a beat.

"Okay. Talk to you later." I was smiling as I hung up; I couldn't help it. "It may be over, Robin," I said, almost crying.

His mouth fell open. "You mean, we don't have to worry anymore?" he asked.

"So it seems. An eyewitness places Benjamin Greer, the member of Real Murders who wasn't there the night Mamie got killed, depositing the briefcase in the culvert. And he has confessed to everything, except sending the candy, which he says Morrison Pettigrue did before he killed him. I'll have to call Mother. Pettigrue thought Mother was a terrible capitalist."

We discussed this truly stunning development up and down and sideways and forwards, until I began to yawn and feel drowsy.

"Did I hear you mention that your brother is coming?" Robin asked tactfully.

"Yes, his name is Phillip, he's six. From my father's remarriage. Dad and his wife are going to a convention in Chattanooga this weekend, and I've been scheduled for a long time to keep Phillip. Things were getting so grim here I was thinking about calling Dad and cancelling or going to keep Phillip at their house, but now I guess it'll be okay to have him here."

"You two get along? What do you do when he's visiting?"

"Oh, we play games. We go to the movies. He watches television. I read to him, things he can't read himself yet. One time we went bowling. That was a real disaster, but fun, too. Sometimes he brings his ball and glove and we play catch in the parking lot. I'm not very good at that, though. Phillip is a real baseball freak, he brings his cards every time he comes and we go through them, while I try not to yawn."

"I like kids," said Robin, and I could tell he was sincere. "Maybe Saturday we can all go to the state park and have a picnic and hike one of the trails."

That would be an hour drive to and from, plus allow maybe three hours for the hike and picnic, I figured rapidly. I could be back in time for roller skating, but Phillip would probably be exhausted from the park, and I might be, too. "Maybe playing—is it called goofy golf?—would be better. I noticed a new place out on the highway into the city when I drove in Monday." That felt years ago now.

"I saw that, too," Robin said. "Maybe Saturday afternoon?"

"Okay, he'll love it. Come meet him tomorrow night," I offered. "I promised to make pecan pie—that's Phillip's favorite. What about 7:00?"

"Great," said Robin agreeably. He leaned over to give me a casual kiss. "I'll see you then." He seemed preoccupied as he left.

I locked the back door after Robin left, and checked my front door, though I seldom used it. If this whole imbroglio had had one effect, it was to make me permanently security conscious.

It had been a busy day even without the constant strain of living with a murderer in close proximity. Today we'd found the hatchet in Robin's briefcase, I'd had the weird confrontation with Gifford Doakes and the eerie scene in the library with Perry. I wondered if Sally was right in her optimistic belief that no one at work besides me had noticed that Perry was unravelling. I hadn't exactly been in the current of office gossip the past week, being mostly the subject of it, I was sure.

Then Arthur had called with the bombshell about Benjamin.

Benjamin the loser. Benjamin the murderer?

As I made up the bed in the guest room for Phillip—though he usually ended up getting spooked at spending the night in a strange place and came in my room—I realized anew how abnormal the week had been. Usually, when I knew Phillip was going to make one of his four or five annual weekend visits, I spent several days preparing. I stocked all his favorite foods, planned lots of activities, checked out an armful of children's books, consulted the local movie schedules. I overdid it.

This was probably the appropriate amount of preparation for a six-year-old's visit; I made a bed for him, checked to see if I had the ingredients for his favorite dessert, and decided to take him to his favorite fast-food place for lunch on Saturday. And I looked forward to seeing him, this unexpected brother I had acquired after I'd become an adult. In the middle of the awfulness I'd seen lately, and the anxiety I'd suffered in so many unprecedented situations, having Phillip to visit seemed like a welcome return to normality.

Benjamin Greer.

I tried to believe it.

SIXTEEN

I WOKE UP SMILING. It took me a second to remember why, but when I remembered, I grinned all over. The murders were at an end. I had convinced myself in my sleep that Benjamin was confessing because he had done it and wanted the attention and infamy, not because he hadn't done it but wanted the attention and infamy anyway. After all, he had announced his candidacy for mayor, that should have given him enough fuel to run on for a while. It was Friday, I didn't have to work this weekend, Phillip was coming, I was interested in two men and what's more they were both interested in me. What more could a twenty-eight-year-old librarian ask for?

I made myself up with great care, had some fun with my eye shadow, and picked my brightest skirt and blouse to wear. It was a definitely springy set, white with yellow flowers scattered all over, and I let my hair hang loose with a yellow band to hold it back.

I had a large breakfast, cereal and toast and even a banana, and sang on my way out to my car.

"You're chipper this morning," said Bankston, who was dressed in a very sober suit befitting a banker. He was smiling himself, and I remembered I'd seen Melanie's car pull out of the parking lot very early this morning.

"Oh, I have reason to be! You may not have heard yet, but someone admitted to the murders."

"Who?" Bankston said after staring at me for a moment.

"Benjamin Greer." Then I wondered belatedly if I was betraying a confidence. But my assurance returned when I remembered Arthur hadn't asked me to keep it quiet, and I hadn't told him I would. Also, I'd already told Robin, who would have throttled the news out of me if I'd hung up from my conversation with Arthur and refused to tell him. Wait; I wasn't even going to say exaggerated things like that to myself anymore.

Bankston was thunderstruck. "But he was just in to see me last week to get a loan for his candidate's campaign! Sorry, I shouldn't have mentioned that. It was a private transaction, bank business. But I'm just so— flabbergasted."

"I was too," I assured him.

"Well, well, I'll have to stop by Melanie's and tell her," he said after a moment of thought. "This will be such a relief to her. She's had a hard time since Mrs. Wright's purse was found in her car."

Right. Being pronounced a martyr at church and getting a marriage proposal was really a hard time. But I felt too cheerful to envy Melanie; I'd gone out with Bankston twice and wouldn't have him on a silver platter, as my mother always said.

Mother. That was someone who should hear the good news, too. I'd call her today. She was going to love being termed "what was worst about capitalism." That was a hard line to take after all Mother's hard work and struggle during the first few years with her business, though then she'd had my father's presence to give her renewed strength. He hadn't left until she was well on the road to success. I was trailing off into unpleasant thoughts, and snapped myself back quickly. Joy was the keynote of the day.

At work, all the librarians and volunteers seemed to have heard the good news, and I was back in the fold. Lillian went back to being her bitchy self, which was almost comforting. Sam Clerrick ventured forth from his charts and graphs and budgets to pat me on the shoulder in passing. I poked book cards in the stamper vigorously, took overdue money with a smile instead of expressionless disapproval, shelved with precision. The morning didn't just hurry by, it hopped, skipped, and jumped by.

The telephone rang twice while I was eating my microwaved egg rolls and browsing through an encyclopedia of twentieth-century murderers. I'd had that familiar irritating feeling that someone, sometime, had said something interesting that I wanted to pursue, mentioned some names I wanted to mull over, and I'd thought flipping through the book would help. But the phone destroyed even this wisp of idea.

The first caller was my father, who always opened with, "How's my doll?"

He hated calling me "Roe" and I hated him calling me "Doll." We hadn't come up with anything neutral. "I'm okay, Dad," I said.

"Is it still okay with you if Phillip comes?" he asked anxiously. "You know, if you are upset about the situation in Lawrenceton, we can stay home."

In the background I could hear Phillip piping anxiously, "Can I go, Daddy? Can I go?"

"The crisis seems to be over," I said happily.

"They arrest someone?"

"They got a confession. I'm sure everything's going to be okay now," I said. Maybe I wasn't all that sure. But I *was* pretty sure that I was going to be okay now. And I wanted to see my little brother.

"Well, I'll be bringing him about five o'clock, then," Dad said. "Betty Jo sends her love. We really appreciate this."

I wasn't so sure about Betty Jo's love, but I was sure she did appreciate having a free, reliable babysitter for a whole weekend.

The next call was from my mother, of course. She still had some sort of psychic link to Dad, and if he called me she nearly always rang within the hour. If she was like Lauren Bacall, he was like Humphrey Bogart; an ugly guy with charisma coming out his ears. And bless his heart, he seemed quite unaware of it. But that charisma was still sending out alpha waves or something to my mother.

I knew that she must already have heard of Benjamin's confession, and sure enough, she had. She'd also heard he'd said Morrison Pettigrue had mailed her the chocolates. She was skeptical.

"How would Morrison Pettigrue hear about Mrs. See's?" she asked. "How would he know I always eat the creams?"

"He didn't have to know you always eat the creams," I pointed out. "There's just no way to get rat poison in the nut-filled ones."

"That's true," she admitted. "I still have a hard time believing that one. I barely knew the man. I'd met him at some Chamber of Commerce meeting once and if I remember correctly, we talked about the need for new sidewalks downtown. It was a cordial conversation and he certainly gave no sign then that he thought I was some kind of leech living off the masses, or whatever."

But if Benjamin was lying about the chocolates, he could also be lying about other things. And I wanted him to be telling the truth and nothing but the truth.

"Let's just shelve this until we find out more about it," I suggested. "Maybe he'll say something that'll make sense out of the whole thing."

"Is—your brother—still staying with you this weekend?" Mother asked, in one of her lightning turns of thought.

I sighed silently. "Yes, Mother. Dad's bringing Phillip by around five, and he'll be here until Sunday evening." It would have been beneath Mother's dignity to avoid the sight of Phillip, but having made a point of talking to him once or twice, she usually stayed away while he was at my place.

"Well, I'll be talking to you again," she was saying now. I could bet on that. I asked her about her business, and she chatted about that for a few minutes.

"Are you and John still thinking about getting married?" I asked.

"Well, we're discussing it." There was a smile in her voice. "I promise you'll be the first to know when we definitely decide."

"As long as I'm the first," I said. "I really am happy for you."

"I hear you have a new beau," Mother said, which was a logical progression when you think about it.

"Which one have you heard about?" I asked, because I simply couldn't resist.

In someone less grand than my mother, I would've called the sound she made a delighted cackle. We hung up with mutual warmth, and I returned to work with the distinct feeling life was on the up and up for me.

MY MOTHER'S "BEAU," John Queensland, came into the library that afternoon while I was on the circulation desk. I realized he was practically the opposite of my father: handsome in an elder-statesman way, and overtly as dignified and reserved as Mother. He had been a widower for some time and still lived in the big two-story house he'd shared with his wife and their two children, both of whom had children of their own now. My contemporaries, I reminded myself gloomily.

As John was checking out two staid biographies of worthy people, he mentioned that his garage had been broken into some time within the last three weeks.

"I never use it anymore, I just park behind the house. The garage is so full of the boys' old stuff—I can't seem to get them to decide what to do with all their junk." He sounded fond rather than complaining. "But anyway, I went to track down my golf clubs since I intended scheduling a game with Bankston in this warmer weather, and the darned thing had been broken into and my golf clubs were gone."

Since John was a Real Murderer, I was sure that this theft meant something. I told John about Gifford Doakes and his hatchet—amazingly, he hadn't heard—and left him to draw his own conclusions.

"I know Benjamin Greer had confessed," I told John, "but that's a bit of evidence the police might need. Just a confession isn't enough, I gather."

"I think I'll go by the police station on my way back to the office," John said thoughtfully. "Those clubs had better be reported. The whole bag was taken, and it was a pretty distinctive set. Every time my kids went somewhere, they got a bumper sticker and put it on my golf bag, just a family joke..." And trailing off with unheard-of-abstraction, John left the library. I thought of Arthur and sighed. I wondered if he'd appreciate being handed another out-of-the-blue fact.

Golf clubs. Maybe they'd already been used. Maybe they'd been used on Mamie. The weapon in that case had never been found, that I knew of. Maybe Benjamin would tell the police where the clubs were.

I let this nag at me until I got home and saw my father's car waiting at my apartment. As I greeted my father and hugged my half-brother, I made a resolution not to think about these killings for a couple of days. I wanted to enjoy Phillip's company.

Phillip is in the first grade and he can be very funny and very exasperating. He will eat about five things with any enthusiasm—five nutritious things, that is. (Anything with no nutritional value whatsoever is always acceptable to Phillip.) Luckily for me, one of those things is spaghetti sauce and another is pecan pie, not that either is exactly a health food.

"Roe! Are we having spaghetti tonight?" he asked eagerly.

"Sure," I said, and smiled at him. I bent and kissed him before he could say, "Yuck! No kisses!" He gave me a quick kiss back, then scrambled to get his suitcase and (much more important) a plastic garbage bag full of essential toys. "I'm going to put these in my room," he told Father, who was beaming at him with unadulterated pride.

"Son, I've got to go now," Father told him. "Your mom is anxious to get where we're going. You be good for your big sister, now, and do what she says to do without giving her any trouble."

Phillip half-listened, mumbled, "Sure, Dad," and lugged his paraphernalia into my place.

"Well, Doll, this sure is nice of you," my father said to me when Phillip had vanished.

"I like Phillip," I said honestly. "I like having him stay here."

"Here are the phone numbers where we'll be staying," Father said and fumbled a sheet of notepaper out of his pocket. "If anything goes wrong, anything at all, call us straight away."

"Okay, okay," I reassured him. "Don't worry. Have a good time. I'll see you Sunday night?"

"Yes, we should be here about five or six. If we're going to be any later than that, we'll call you. Don't forget to remind him about his prayers. Oh—if he runs a fever or anything, here's a box of chewable children's aspirin. He gets three. And he needs to have a glass of water by the bed at night."

"I'll remember." We hugged, and he got in his car with a lopsided smile and half-wave that I could see a woman would have a hard time forgetting. I watched Father drive out of the parking lot, and then heard Phillip shouting from the kitchen, "Roe! You got any cookies?"

I supplied Phillip with two awful sandwich cookies that he'd told me were his favorites. Very pleased, he bounced outside with his garbage bag of toys, having dumped the "inside" ones in the middle of my den. "I bet you have to cook, so I'm going to be out here playing," he said seriously.

I could take a hint. I got busy with the spaghetti sauce.

The next time I glanced out the window to check, I saw through my open patio gate that Phillip had already commandeered Bankston into playing baseball in the parking lot. Phillip had great scorn for my baseball playing ability, but Bankston had his approval. Bankston had taken off his suit coat and his tie immediately, and seemed not nearly so stuffy as he pitched the baseball to Phillip's waiting bat. They'd played before when Phillip had visited, and Bankston didn't seem to consider it an imposition.

Then Robin was drawn into the game when he got home, and he was acting as Phillip's catcher when I called from the patio gate that supper was ready.

"Yahoo!" Phillip shrieked, and propped his bat against the patio wall. I smiled and shrugged at his abandoned playmates and whispered to Phillip, "Thank Bankston and Robin for a good game." "Thank you," Phillip said obediently and dashed in to scramble into his chair at my small dining table. I glimpsed the top of Melanie's head in Bankston's open door as he went in, and Robin said, "See you later, for pecan pie. I like you little brother," as he strolled through the gate to his patio. I felt warm and flushed with pride at having such a cute brother—and a little warm too at Robin's smile, which had definitely been of the personal variety.

For the next twenty minutes I was occupied in seeing that Phillip used his napkin and said his prayer and ate at least a little serving of vegetables. I looked fondly at his perpetually tousled light brown hair and his startlingly blue eyes, so different from mine. Between bites of spaghetti and garlic bread, Phillip was telling me a long involved story about a fight on the school playground, involving a boy whose brother really knew karate and another boy who really had all the G.I. Joe attack vehicles. I listened with half an ear, the other part of my mind being increasingly occupied by the niggling feeling that I was supposed to know something. Or remember something. Or had I seen something? Whatever this "something" was, I needed to call it to mind.

"My baseball!" shrieked Phillip suddenly.

He had my full attention. The shriek, which had sprung with no warning from his throat while he was telling me what the principal had done to the playground combatants, had scared the whosis out of me.

"But Phillip, it's dark," I protested, as he catapulted out of his chair and dashed to the back door. I tried to remember if I'd ever seen him walk, and decided that I had, once, when he was about twelve-months-old. "Here, at least take my flashlight!"

I managed to stuff it in his hand only because he was so partial to flashlights that he slowed down long enough for me to pull it from the kitchen cabinet.

"And try to remember where you last saw the ball!" I bellowed after him.

I'd finished my meal while Phillip was relating his long story, so I scraped my plate and put it in the dishwasher (Robin was due in a few minutes, and I wanted the place to look neat). The dessert plates were out, everything else was ready, so while I waited for a triumphant Phillip to return with his baseball, I idly looked at my shelves, putting a few books back in place that were out of order. I stared at the titles of all those books about bad or crazy or crazed people, men and women whose lives had crossed the faint line that demarks those who could but haven't from those who can and have.

Phillip had been gone a long time; I couldn't hear him out in the parking lot.

The phone rang.

"Yes?" I said abruptly into the receiver.

"Roe, it's Sally Allison."

"What..."

"Have you seen Perry?"

"What? No!"

"Has he been . . . following you anymore?"

"No... at least, I haven't noticed if he has."

"He..." Sally trailed off.

"Come on, Sally! What's the matter?" I asked roughly. I stared out through the kitchen window, hoping to see the beam of the flashlight bobbing around through the slats in the patio fence. I remembered the night Perry'd been across the street in the dark waiting for Robin to bring me home. I was terrified.

"He didn't take his medicine today. He didn't go to work. I don't know where he is. Maybe he took some more pills."

"Call the police, then. Get them looking for him, Sally! What if he's here? My little brother's out alone in the dark!" I hung up the phone with a hysterical bang. I grabbed up my huge key ring, with some idea of taking my car around the block for a search, and I pulled out the second flashlight I kept ready.

It was my fault. The thing in the dark had gotten my little brother, a six-year-old child, and it was *my fault*. Oh Lord God, heavenly King, protect the child.

I left the back door wide open, the welcome light spilling into the deep dusk. The patio gate was already open, Phillip never remembered to close it. His bat was propped beside it as he'd left it coming in to supper.

"Phillip!" I screamed. Then I thought, maybe I should be quiet and creep. In a frenzy of indecision, I swung the flashlight to and fro. A few yards away, a car started up and pulled out of its space. As it went by, I saw it was Melanie in Bankston's car. She smiled and waved. I gaped after her. How could she not have heard me yell?

But I couldn't reason, I just kept walking and sweeping the ground with that beam of light, seeing nothing, nothing.

"Roe, what's wrong? I was just on my way over to your place!" Robin loomed above me in the dark.

"Phillip's gone, someone's got him! He left to get his baseball, he ran out the back door, he didn't come back!"

"I'll get a flashlight," Robin said instantly. He turned to go to his telephone. "Listen—" he half-turned back but kept moving, "he wouldn't think it was funny to hide, would he?"

"I don't think so," I said. I would have loved to have thought Phillip was giggling behind a bush somewhere, but I knew he wasn't. He couldn't have stayed hidden this long in the dark. He'd have jumped out long before, screaming "boo," his grin of triumph making his face shine. "Listen, Robin, go ask the Crandalls if they've seen Phillip, and call the police. Perry Allison's mom just called and he's loose somewhere. She may not call the police. I'm going to work my way around to search the front yard."

"Right," Robin said briefly, and vanished into his place.

I walked quickly through the dark (and it was full dark now), the beam of the flashlight on the sidewalk before me. I'd pause, and swing the flashlight, and step on. I passed the Crandalls' gate, and had found nothing. I opened Bankston's gate. The flashlight beam caught something on Bankston's patio.

Phillip's baseball.

Oh, God, it had been here all the time, no wonder Phillip couldn't find it. Bankston had probably picked it up out of the parking lot to keep it to give Phillip tomorrow morning.

I lifted my hand to knock on Bankston's back door and my hand froze in midair. I thought about Melanie pulling out of the parking lot so strangely—she must have heard me scream.

And I'd told Phillip to think of where he'd seen it last. He'd seen it last in Bankston's hands.

Had Bankston been lying down in that car? Had he been lying on top of Phillip, to keep him quiet?

A long brown hair had been found in the Bucklcys' house. Benjamin didn't have long brown hair. He had thinning blond hair. Like Bankston. He was medium height, like Bankston, and he had a round face. Like Bankston. It was Bankston the young mother had seen in the alley, not Benjamin Greer.

Melanie had long brown hair. *Together.* They had done the killings together.

And then I remembered that niggly little thing that had been bothering me. When John Queensland had described his golf bag, he'd said it had stickers all over it. That had been the golf bag Bankston was carrying into his place on Wednesday, so long after my lunch hour he hadn't expected me to be around at all, much less popping out of the Crandalls' gate. Bankston had stolen them from John Queensland.

Had Phillip been in Bankston's townhouse? I turned my flashlight on my key ring. You couldn't call it breaking and entering, I told myself hysterically. I had a key. I was the landlady. I turned it in the keyhole, opened the door as quietly as I could, and stepped inside.

I didn't call out. I left the back door open.

The kitchen light was on, and the kitchen/living room was a mess, but an ordinary mess. A library book was lying open on the counter, a book I had in my own personal library, Emlyn Williams' *Beyond Belief*. I felt sick, and had to bend over.

This time they were patterning themselves after Myra Hindley and Ian Brady, the "Moors Murderers." They were going to kill a child. They were going to kill my brother. The monster was not sitting in a jail cell in the Lawrenceton City Jail. The monsters lived here.

Hindley and Brady had tortured the children for a few hours first, so Phillip might be alive. If he'd been in the car, if they'd taken him to Melanie's place, wherever that was—right, the same street where Jane Engle lived—he might have left some trace.

Abandoning silence, I raced up the stairs. No one. In the larger bedroom there was a king-sized bed with a coil of rope beside it, and a camera was on the dresser.

Hindley and Brady, two low-level office workers who'd met on the job, had tape-recorded and photographed their victims.

The extra bedroom was full of exercise equipment: the source of Bankston's newly bulging muscles. There was a file box with its lid hanging back, key still in the lock. Anything he locked up, I wanted to see. I knocked it over and the magazines inside spilled out like a trail of slime. I looked at one open one in horror. I did not know it was possible to buy pictures of women being treated like that. When I had heard of the anti-pornography movement, I'd thought of the usual pictures of women who at least were apparently willing, being paid, and still healthy when the photo session was over.

I ran back downstairs, glanced into the living room, opened the closets. Nothing. I opened the door to the basement. The light was off, so the steps were dark from halfway down to the bottom. But something white was on one of the lower steps, just visible in the light spilling down from the kitchen.

I went down the stairs and crouched to pick it up. It was a baseball card.

I heard a muffled noise, and had time to think, Phillip! But then I felt a terrible pain across my shoulder and neck, and I was falling forward, my arms and legs tangled, my face scraping the edge of the steps. The next thing I knew I was on the floor of the basement and looking up at Bankston's face, stolid no more in the dim light but grinning like a gargoyle, and he had a golf club in his hand.

There was another switch at the bottom of the steps, and he turned it on. I heard the noise again, and with great pain turned my head to see Phillip, gagged and with his hands tied, sitting on a straight chair by the dryer. His face was wet with tears and his whole little body was curled into as tight a ball as he could manage in that chair. His feet could not touch the floor.

My heart broke.

I'd heard people say that all my life; their heart had broken because their love had deserted them, their heart had broken because their cat had died, their heart had broken because they'd dropped Grandma's vase.

I was going to die and I had cost my little brother his life, and my heart broke for what he would endure before they finally tired of him and killed him.

"We heard you come in," Bankston said, smiling. "We were down here waiting for you, weren't we, Phillip?"

Incredible, Bankston the banker. Bankston with the matching almond-tone washer and dryer. Bankston arranging a loan for a businessman in the afternoon and smashing Mamie Wright's face in the evening. Melanie the secretary, filling up her idle time while her boss was out of town by slaughtering the Buckleys with a hatchet. The perfect couple.

Phillip was crying hopelessly. "Shut up, Phillip," said the man who'd played baseball with him that afternoon. "Every time you cry, I'll hit your sister. Won't I, sis?" and the golf club whistled through the air and Bankston broke my collarbone. My shriek must have covered Melanie's steps, because suddenly she was there looking down at me with pleasure.

"When I pulled in, the Scarecrow was searching the parking lot," she said to Bankston. "Here's the tape recorder. I can't believe we forgot it!"

Gee, what a madcap couple. She sounded for all the world like a housewife who'd remembered the potato salad in the fridge just as the family was leaving on its picnic.

I decided, when the pain had ebbed enough for me to think, that "the Scarecrow" was Robin. I managed to look at Phillip again. God bless him, he was trying so hard not to make sounds, so Bankston wouldn't hit me again. I tried to push the pain away so I could look reassuring, but I could only stare at him and try not to scream myself. If I screamed, Bankston would hit me quite a lot.

Or maybe he would hit Phillip.

"What do you think?" Bankston asked her.

"No way we can get them out of here now," Melanie said matter-of-factly. "He said he'd called the police. One of us better go up soon and offer to help search. If we don't the police will want to look in here, I guess, get suspicious. We can't have that, can we?" and she smiled archly, and poked my leg with her foot, as if I were a piece of naughtiness that they had to conceal for convention's sake. She saw me looking at her. "Get up and get over there by the kid," she said, and then she kicked me. I moaned. "I've always wanted to do that," she said to Bankston with a smile.

It was not only the fall and the blows that made it hard to move, but the shock. I was in this most prosaic basement with these most prosaic people, and they were monsters that were going to kill me, me and my brother. I had read and marvelled for years at people living cheek by jowl with psychopaths, and not suspecting. And here I was, trying desperately to crawl across a concrete floor in a building my mother owned while friends looked for my brother outside, because I had never never thought it could happen to me. I got to Phillip's side in a few moments, though the young woman I'd known all my life and gone to church with did kick me a few times on the journey. I grabbed the edge of the seat and dragged myself to my knees, and clumsily draped my good arm around Phillip. I wished Phillip would faint. His face was more than I could stand, and I had no consolation for him. We were looking at the faces of demons, and all the rules of kindness and courtesy that Phillip and I had been taught so carefully did not apply. No reward for good behavior.

"I got the tape recorder, but now we can't use it," Melanie was pouting. "I think that's when she got suspicious, when she saw me pull out of the parking lot. I didn't want to have to help her look, so I had to act like I didn't hear her. I don't guess we'll get to have any fun tonight."

"I didn't think this through," Bankston agreed. "Now they'll be out there looking for the boy and her all night, and we'll have to go volunteer, too. At least now we've got her keys, they can't use the master set to come in here." He held them up. I must have dropped them when I fell.

"You think they might insist on searching all the apartments?" Melanie asked anxiously. "We can't turn them down if they ask."

Bankston pondered. They were at the foot of the steps still. I could not get by them. I could not see any weapons besides the golf club, but even if I did attack them with my one good arm and my little remaining energy, the two of them could easily overcome me and the noise would not be heard by anyone... unless the Crandalls had decided to spend the evening in their basement. "We'll just have to wing it," Bankston said finally.

The baseball! Maybe Robin would see it, like I had.

"Did you talk to anyone when you pulled in?" Bankston was asking.

"Just what I told you before. Robin asked me if I had seen the boy, and I said no, but that I'd be glad to help look," Melanie said with no irony whatsoever. "Roe left the back door open, so I closed and re-locked it. And I picked up the kid's baseball, it was still out on the patio."

That was our death warrant, I reckoned.

Bankston cursed. "How did it end up out there? I was sure I'd brought it in."

"Don't worry about it," Melanie said. "Even if they did find it, you could just have said you'd been keeping it for him but he didn't ever show up looking for it."

"You're right," Bankston said fondly. "What shall we do with those two? If we leave them tied up down here while we go help to search, they might somehow get loose. If we kill them right now, we lose our fun with the boy." He strolled over to us and Melanie followed.

"You acted on impulse when you grabbed him," Melanie observed. "We should just go on and take care of them now, and hide them down here good. Then when the search dies down, we'll see if we can get them out to the car and dump them. Next time, no impulses, we'll do what we planned and nothing extra."

"Are you criticizing me?" Bankston asked sharply. His voice was low and dangerous.

Her posture changed. I had never seen anything like it. She cringed and folded and became another person. "No, never," she whimpered, and she bent and licked his hand. I saw her eyes, and she was role-playing and it excited her immensely.

I was nauseated. I hoped I was blocking Phillip's view sufficiently. I huddled closer to him, though the pain from my collarbone was becoming more insistent. Phillip was shaking and he had wet himself. His breath was getting more and more ragged, and muffled sobs and whimpers broke out from time to time.

Melanie and Bankston were giving each other a kiss, and Bankston bent and bit her shoulder. She held him to her as though they would use each other right there, but then they unclenched and she said, "We'd better do it now. Why run any more risks?"

"You're right," Bankston agreed. He gave her the golf club, and she swung it through the air experimentally while he searched his pockets. In her black slacks and green sweater and knotted scarf she looked ready to tee off at the country club. In that small area the club whistled past me with no room to spare, and I started to protest, when I realized yet again that Melanie absolutely could not care less. Old assumptions die hard.

I saw a foot on the stairs behind them.

"Give me your scarf, Mel," Bankston said suddenly. Melanie unknotted it instantly. "This would be less messy, and I've never done it before," he observed cheerfully. They never looked at me or at Phillip, except in passing, and I could tell to them we were not people like they were.

The foot was joined by a matching foot, and silently took another step down.

"Maybe I should tape this," Melanie said brightly. "It won't be what we had planned, but it might be interesting."

The next step squeaked, and I screamed, "God damn you to hell! How can you do this to me? How can you do this to a little boy?"

They were as shocked as though a chair had spoken. Melanie swung the club instantly with both hands. My body was covering Phillip's on the chair, but the blow was so strong the chair was rocked. It was easy to shriek as loud as a freight train. I saw the feet descend all the way in a rush.

"Shut up, bitch!" Melanie said furiously.

"Naw, you shut up," a flat voice advised her.

It was old Mr. Crandall, and he was carrying a very large gun.

The only sound in the basement was the sobbing coming from me, as I struggled to control myself. Phillip raised his bound wrists to loop his arms over my head. I wished more than ever that he'd faint.

"You're not going to shoot," Bankston said. "You old idiot. With this concrete floor, it'll ricochet and hit them."

"I'd rather shoot them directly than leave them to you," Mr. Crandall said simply.

"Which one of us will you shoot first?" Melanie asked furiously. She'd been sidling away from Bankston a little at a time. "You can't get us both, old man."

"But I can," said Robin from higher on the stairs, and he wasn't nearly as calm as Mr. Crandall. I managed to look up. I saw Robin descending with a shotgun. "Now I don't know as much about guns as Mr. Crandall, but he loaded this for me, and if I point it and fire I am real sure I will hit something."

If they tried anything desperate it would be now. I could feel the turmoil pouring from them. They looked at each other. I could only stare through a haze of pain at the green silk scarf in Bankston's hand. Oh, surely they must see it was over, over.

Suddenly the fight oozed out of them. They looked like what they used to be, for a moment; a bank loan officer and a secretary, who could not remember where they were or how they had come to be there.

The scarf fell from Bankston's hand. Melanie lay down the golf club. They did not look at each other anymore.

There was a gust of people noise, and Arthur and Lynn Liggett came pelting down the stairs to be stopped short by the tableau.

Phillip's breath came out from behind the gag in a deep sigh, and he fainted. It seemed like such a good idea that I did it, too.

SEVENTEEN

"If I'D HAD MY Dynamite Man Particle Blaster they wouldn't have hurt us," Phillip whispered. He simply would not be parted from me while I was being patched up. He held on to my hand or my leg or my torso; though many kind people offered to take him and rock him, or buy him an ice cream cone, or color with him, my little brother would not be separated from me. This definitely made it harder on me, but I tried to have so much sympathy for Phillip that the pain would not seem important. I'm afraid I found that to me, pain is very important, no matter who else has been hurt.

Now he was actually in the hospital bed with me, huddling as close to me as he could get, his eyes still wide and staring, but beginning to glaze over. I thought he'd had some kind of mild tranquilizer; I thought I remembered saying that was okay. My father and stepmother were driving back from Chattanooga; Robin, bless him, had found their phone number and called, miraculously catching them in their motel room.

"Phillip, if I hadn't had you to hold on to, I would have gone nuts," I assured him. "You were so brave.

I know you were scared inside, like I was, but you were brave as a lion to hold yourself together.''

"I was thinking about escaping all the time. I was just waiting for a chance,'' he informed me. There, he was beginning to sound more like Phillip. Then, less certainly, "Roe, would they really have killed us?''

What was I supposed to say? I glanced over at Robin, who shrugged in an it's-up-to-you gesture. Why was I asking Robin what I should say to my little brother?

"Yes,'' I said, and took a deep breath. "Yes, they were really bad people. They were rotten apples. They were nice on the outside but full of worms on the inside.''

"But they're locked up in jail now?''

"You bet.'' I thought about lawyers and bail and I shivered. Surely not. "They can't ever get you again. They can't ever hurt anybody again. They're far away and all locked up, and your mom and dad will carry you home even farther away from them.''

"When are they gonna get here?'' he asked desolately.

"Soon, soon, as fast as their car can come,'' I said as soothingly as I could, perhaps for the fiftieth time, and thank God at that moment my father did come in, Betty Jo right behind him and under rigid control.

"Mama!'' said Phillip, and all his hard-held toughness left him. He became an instant soggy puddle of little boy. Betty Jo swept him out of the hospital bed and into her arms and held him as tightly as he held her. "Where can I take him?" she asked the nurse who'd followed them in. The nurse told her about an empty waiting room two doors down, and Betty Jo vanished with her precious armful. I was so glad to see Betty Jo take him I could have cried. There is no substitute for a real mother. At least I am no substitute for a real mother. The past few hours had certainly taught me that, if I'd ever doubted it.

My father bent and kissed me. "I hear you saved his life," he said, and tears trickled down his face. I had never seen my father cry. "I am so thankful you are both safe, I prayed in the car all the way here. I could have lost both of you in one night." Overwhelmed, he sank into the guest chair Robin had quietly vacated. Robin stood back in the shadows, the dim room light glinted off his red hair. I would never forget how he'd looked with the shotgun in his hands.

I was just too tired to appreciate my father's emotion. It was late, so late. I had almost been strangled by a bank loan officer with a green silk scarf. I had been hit by a secretary with a golf club. I had been terrified out of my mind for myself and my little brother. I had looked into the face of evil. Strong words, I told myself hazily, but true. The face of evil.

Finally, my dear father dried his eyes, told me he'd see me very soon, and said they were taking Phillip home that very night. "We'll have to see about treatment for him," he said apprehensively. "I don't know how to help him."

"I'll see you," I mumbled.

"Thanks, Aurora," he said. "If you need help yourself, you know how to reach us." But they were dying to get Phillip away, and his voice verged on perfunctory. I was a grownup, right? I could take care of myself. Or my mother would take care of me. I let myself have a flash of bitterness, and made myself swallow it. He was not being careful of me, but he was right.

I drifted off to sleep for a second. Robin was holding my hand when I woke up. I think he had kissed me.

"That felt good," I said. So he did it again. It felt even better.

"They were stupid really," I said a little later.

"When you think about it, yes," Robin agreed. "I don't think they ever realized it wasn't a game when they began patterning the deaths after old murders. Bankston snatched Phillip on impulse when they should have waited and picked a victim from at least across town...if he'd really been intelligent, he would have known taking Phillip from the same place he himself lived, then keeping him in the townhouse instead of getting him out to Melanie's place...well, maybe they would've smuggled him out, but you started looking too soon, and they didn't even consider you having keys."

"How did you know where we were?" I asked. It had never occurred to me to question our last-minute rescue.

"When I saw Melanie pull back in, she acted strange," he began. "I had started to wonder where you'd disappeared, too, and her coming back after she'd just left a few minutes before seemed peculiar. She'd gone home to get her tape recorder, you know," he said, and looked away into the shadows of the room. "I ran around front, saw you weren't there searching, and decided there was only one place you could be. Really, I was just guessing," he said frankly. "You had disappeared as suddenly as Phillip, there were no strange cars around, Melanie tried to act concerned about Phillip being missing but she wasn't, and she had that damn tape recorder. Perry Allison is very strange and maybe dangerous, but he's also obvious." Robin reached down to take my hand. "I had to persuade Mr. Crandall in a hurry that we had to raid Bankston's place, but he was game. Even if I had made a mistake, he said, if Bankston was any kind of a man he would realize when a child and woman are missing, anything goes. Jed's a frontier kind of guy."

"How'd you get in? Didn't Melanie lock the door behind her?"

"Yes, but Mrs. Crandall had a key, the key she'd been meaning to bring over to you—I think she kept it because the former tenant used to lock herself out a lot."

I would have laughed if my side hadn't hurt so much. The emergency room doctor said I'd be able to go home in the next day or two, but my collarbone and two ribs were broken, and I was bruised all over from tumbling down the stairs. There was a spectacularly ugly combination of bruise and scrape covering one cheek.

My mother wanted me to come home with her, but I was going to tell her I'd rather be in my own place, I decided, depending on how sore I was in the morning. Mother had flown into the hospital with every eyelash in place but a wild look in those fine eyes. We had hugged and talked for a while, and she had even shed a few tears (certainly atypical), but when she learned that as far as I knew my apartment was sitting wide open and, for that matter, Bankston's as well since the police were still searching it, she decided I was well enough to leave and flew off to see to safeguarding my property and the disposition of Bankston's.

My mother was a friend of Bankston's mother, and she was terrified of seeing Mrs. Waites again. "That poor woman," Mother said. "How can she live with having raised a monster like that? The other Waites children are fine people. What happened? He's known you all your life, Aurora! How could he hurt you? How could he think of hurting a child?"

"Who knows?" I said wearily. "He was having a great time, the time of his life." I had no sympathy to spare for Bankston's mother, right now. I had no extra emotion of any kind to throw around. I was drained, exhausted, and in pain. I had bruises and bandages galore. Even Robin's kiss didn't make me feel lecherous, just raised the possibility that someday I might feel that way. He was picking up his jacket now, getting ready to go.

"Robin," I murmured. I seemed to be drifting down into sleep. He turned, and I realized that he was spent, too. His tall shoulders were stooped, the crinkly mouth drooping down at the corners. Even his flaming hair looked limp.

"You saved me," I said.

"Nah, Jed Crandall saved you," he said with an attempt at being off-hand. "I was just back-up muscle."

"You saved me. Thank you." And then I drifted down a long spiral into sleep.

When I woke up again the clock said 3:30 A.M. Someone else was sitting in the guest chair, someone short and stocky and blond and fast asleep. Arthur's head was slumped forward on his chest and he was snoring a little. I'd have to remember that.

My mouth was dry and my throat sore, so I reached for the cup of water on the bedside table. Naturally, it was just out of reach. I wiggled painfully sideways, still stretching, but then Arthur handed it to me.

"I didn't want to wake you up," I told him.

"I was just dozing," he said quietly.

"What happened?"

"Well, we found a box of—mementoes—at Melanie Clark's little rented house."

"Mementoes?" I asked with dread.

"Yes. Pictures."

I shook my head. I didn't want to hear more.

He nodded. "Pretty awful. They photographed Mamie and the Buckleys after they died. And Morrison Pettigrue. Melanie made advances to him, it turns out, and she got him to get undressed that way. Then she killed him, and let Bankston in, and they arranged him."

"So they confessed?"

"Well, Bankston did. He was proud."

"So they weren't like Hindley and Brady in the end."

"No. Melanie tried to kill herself."

"Oh," I said after a moment. "Oh, no."

"We had a watch on them both, so we caught her fairly quickly. She had taken off her bra and was trying to hang herself with it."

So grotesque, but at least it showed human feeling.

"She was sorry," I said softly.

"No," Arthur said definitely. Sharply. "She didn't want to be separated from Bankston."

There seemed to be nothing to say. I handed my cup back to Arthur, who put it on the beside table and automatically refilled it.

"They were mad we hadn't found the weapon Bankston used to kill Mamie Wright. They were sure they'd planted it where we couldn't help but find it. It was a hammer they'd stolen from LeMaster Cane's garage, and it had his initials on it. But as it turns out, some kids had picked it up the same night they killed her, and the kids only got scared and turned it in tonight. Evidently Melanie and Bankston were going to use the golf clubs in the future. After you saw Bankston carrying them into his place—he'd just showered over at Melanie's after killing the Buckleys, and he was going to get the clubs out of his car at a time when he thought no one would be out and about at the apartments—he got scared and ditched the bag, the only distinctive thing about the set, the next dark night. But he kept one or two of the clubs on the off-chance he might need a weapon. Then you and Crusoe found the briefcase... we fell down on that one. I don't mind telling you, we wondered about Crusoe for a while after that. Tonight I was ready to shoot him when I saw him charging into Waites's place with a shotgun, but Jed Crandall's wife was running out of her gate saying, "My husband and Mr. Crusoe have gone down in Bankston Waites's basement to catch the murderer!" I was half expecting to see Perry Allison down in that basement, standing over Waites's body, and yours, and Phillip's."

"Where is Perry? Does anyone know?" It was Sally's call that had sent me running out in the dark soon enough to raise the alarm so Bankston and Melanie hadn't a chance to get Phillip away.

"He's checked himself into a mental hospital in the city," Arthur said.

That was undoubtedly the place for him, but it would be hard on Sally.

"Benjamin?"

"We're sending him to State Psychiatric for evaluation. He also confessed to several other murders we'd definitely solved. Somehow finding Pettigrue's body unhinged him.''

"Oh, Arthur," I said wearily, and began to cry for so many different reasons I couldn't count them. Arthur stuffed tissues in my hand, and after a while brought over a wet washrag and wiped my face very carefully.

"I guess roller skating tomorrow night is off?" Arthur asked seriously.

I gaped at him in shock until I realized that Arthur—of all people!—was making a joke. I couldn't help smiling. It slid all around my face, but it was a smile.

"I've got to go back to the station, Roe. They're still sorting through the stuff they found in the search, and there's a lot we don't know yet. How Bankston got Mamie Wright to come to the meeting early. Why he let Melanie mail you that candy. He'd bought it for her and brought it back from some convention in St. Louis. But she had it in for you in a big way, and she thought you were the one who liked chocolate creams. That was the stupidest crime, since the typewriter's sitting in Gerald Wright's insurance office. We need to ask more questions, so we can back up these confessions with some solid evidence. Bankston has waived his right to have a lawyer present, but sooner or later he's gonna regret it and that'll be the end of the confession. Back to work for me."

"Okay, Arthur. I was glad to see you come down the stairs tonight."

"I was glad to see you alive."

"It was close."

"I know." Then he bent over and kissed me, and I thought I was getting to be quite a hussy.

"I'll be back tomorrow," he promised, and then he was gone, and for the first time in forever I was alone. I was exhausted to the bone, but I could not sleep. I was afraid to close my eyes.

I turned on the television to CNN, to find that I was on it. They were using a picture I'd had made when I joined the library staff. I looked impossibly sweet and young.

I was on the news. I'd be in the books when this case joined others in accounts of true murder cases. I had seen real murderers and I had almost been really murdered. That was something to ponder. I flicked the remote control to off.

I thought of Bankston and Melanie coming into the VFW Hall that night, disappointed to see me, maybe, since they expected I would have received and eaten the chocolate by that time. And I could see them waiting, waiting, for someone there to go looking for Mamie Wright. I remembered how fresh from the shower Bankston had looked when he was carrying in the stolen golf bag the day the Buckleys had been slaughtered. He'd been so shiny and clean...I had never, never suspected him. I heard Melanie's voice as she'd said, "I've always wanted to do this," and kicked me.

It was too close, too recent, I'd been frightened too deeply.

Of course, this hadn't turned out to be a real puzzler, like the 1928 intrafamilial poisonings in Croyden, England, unsolved to this day. Was Mrs. Duff guilty? . . . or could it have been . . . I drifted away in sleep.

BARBARA PAUL
IN-LAWS
and OUTLAWS

Gillian Clifford, once a Decker in-law, returns to the family fold to comfort Raymond's widow, Connie. Clearly, the family is worried. Who hates the Deckers enough to kill them?

And as the truth behind the murder becomes shockingly clear, Gillian realizes that once a Decker, always a Decker—a position she's discovering can be most precarious indeed.

 WORLDWIDE LIBRARY®

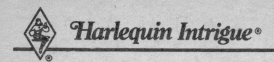
Harlequin Intrigue ®

Trust No One...

When you are outwitting a cunning killer, confronting dark secrets
or unmasking a devious imposter, it's hard to know whom to trust.
Strong arms reach out to embrace you—but are they a safe
harbor...or a tiger's den?

When you're on the run, do you dare to fall in love?

For heart-stopping suspense and heart-stirring romance, read
Harlequin Intrigue.

HARLEQUIN INTRIGUE—where you can expect the unexpected.

INTRIGUE-R

OTHER PEOPLE'S HOUSES

SUSAN ROGERS COOPER

In Prophesy County, Oklahoma, the unlikely event of a homicide is coupled with the likely event that if one occurs, the victim is somebody everybody knows....

And everybody knows nice bank teller Lois Bell who, along with her husband and three kids, dies of accidental carbon monoxide poisoning. But things just aren't sitting right with chief deputy Milton Kovak. Why were the victims' backgrounds completely untraceable? And why was the federal government butting its nose in the case?

"Milt Kovak tells his story with a voice that's as comforting as a rocking chair and as salty as a fisherman."

—*Houston Chronicle*